Animals in Our Days

Middle East Literature in Translation
Michael Beard and Adnan Haydar, *Series Editors*

Animals in Our Days

A Book of Stories

Mohamed Makhzangi

Translated from the Arabic by
Chip Rossetti

Syracuse University Press

This book was originally published in Arabic
as *Ḥayawanāt Ayyāmnā* (Cairo: Dār al-Shurūq, 2006).

Copyright © 2022 by Chip Rossetti
Syracuse University Press
Syracuse, New York 13244-5290

First Edition 2022

22   23   24   25   26   27   6   5   4   3   2   1

∞ The paper used in this publication meets the minimum requirements
of the American National Standard for Information Sciences—Permanence
of Paper for Printed Library Materials, ANSI Z39.48-1992.

For a listing of books published and distributed by Syracuse University Press,
visit www.press.syr.edu.

ISBN: 978-0-8156-1148-6 (paperback)   978-0-8156-5562-6 (e-book)

Library of Congress Cataloging-in-Publication Data

Names: Makhzanjī, Muḥammad, author. | Rossetti, Chip, translator.
Title: Animals in our days : a book of stories / Mohamed Makhzangi ;
    translated from the Arabic by Chip Rossetti.
Other titles: Hayawānāt ayyāminā. English
Description: First edition. | Syracuse : Syracuse University Press, 2022. |
    Series: Middle East literature in translation | Includes bibliographical
    references. | Summary: "A themed collection of short stories about
    animals, which offers a striking example of environmentally concerned
    literature from the Arab world, by an Egyptian author with a keen and
    sensitive eye for the behavior of animals—especially homo sapiens"—
    Provided by publisher. Identifiers: LCCN 2021054384 (print) |
    LCCN 2021054385 (ebook) | ISBN 9780815611486 (paperback) |
    ISBN 9780815655626 (ebook)
Subjects: LCSH: Animals—Fiction. | LCGFT: Short stories.
Classification: LCC PJ7846.A4949 H3913 2022 (print) | LCC PJ7846.
    A4949(ebook) | DDC 808.83/9362—dc23/eng/20211109
LC record available at https://lccn.loc.gov/2021054384
LC ebook record available at https://lccn.loc.gov/2021054385

Manufactured in the United States of America

For John, who loves animals
—CR

Contents

Translator's Introduction
On Homo Sapiens *and Other Species*

Mohamed Makhzangi's *Animals in Our Days* (original Arabic title: *Ḥayawanāt Ayyāmnā*) offers a striking example of environmentally concerned literature in Arabic, by an author with a keen and sensitive eye for the behavior of animals, including—or perhaps, especially—*Homo sapiens*. Originally published in 2006, this themed collection revolves around animals, without resorting to anthropomorphism or sentimentality. Each story focuses on a different animal species, whether water buffalo driven mad by a rural village oversaturated with electric lights, brass grasshoppers bought in a crowded Bangkok marketplace, or ghostly rabbits that haunt the site of a brutal military crackdown that took place decades before. In these tales, animals highlight the brutality and callousness of humanity, particularly when technology and capitalism sunder the ties between people and the natural world around them.

In the field of contemporary Egyptian letters, Mohamed Makhzangi is known not only for his fiction, but for his long career in science journalism. Born in 1949 in the city of Mansoura in Egypt's Delta region, Makhzangi attended medical school in Cairo and trained as a psychiatrist. His political activism while he attended university coincided with Egypt's leftist student movement. The student movement had emerged in 1968 as an expression of frustration with the Nasserist regime following the 1967 war, and it was increasingly repressed by Anwar Sadat's government over the course of the 1970s.[1] In January 1977 Makhzangi was imprisoned for his political activism, when he, along with other university students, was accused of having instigated Egypt's widespread bread riots.[2] In the mid-1980s, he lived in Kiev, Ukraine, continuing his studies in psychology and in alternative medicine. He was living there at the time of the Chernobyl nuclear accident in 1986, an experience that formed the basis for a memoir, *Laḥẓāt gharaq*

1. See Ahmed Abdalla, *The Student Movement and National Politics in Egypt: 1923–1973* (London: Saqi Books, 1985). For a personal account of the same era, see Arwa Salih, *The Stillborn: Notebooks of a Woman from the Student-Movement Generation in Egypt*, trans. Samah Selim (London: Seagull Books, 2018).

2. Mohamed Makhzangi, "Naʿm li-l-tamarrud, lā li-qatlah," *Al-Shurūq*, June 13, 2013, https://www.shorouknews.com /columns/view.aspx?cdate=13062013&id=da0da1ec-fc2d-4eca -ab9c-fff2576e7ae5.

jazīrat al-ḥūt (translated as *Memories of a Melt-down*), and led to his becoming one of Egypt's most prominent antinuclear activists. After twelve years of practicing medicine, he turned to writing, following the same career path as another notable Egyptian physician-turned-author, Yusuf Idris. For a number of years, Makhzangi lived in Kuwait, where he served as the science editor for *al-'Arabī* magazine, which is now based in Egypt. He has authored ten short-story collections (two of them for children, including a 2010 collection of thirty-three stories on animals and nature),[3] as well as books on travel and other nonfiction. He has also won two major Egyptian literary awards for his fiction.

First published in 2006, *Animals in Our Days* encompasses many of the themes and preoccupations that have marked Makhzangi's writings throughout his career: a keen observation of the natural world, global settings that reflect the author's wide-ranging travels across Africa and Asia, and a generous sympathy for the weak and downtrodden, whether human or animal.

The emphasis in these stories on animal species and humans' often cruel and thoughtless behavior toward them places this work within the literary genre of ecofiction, a broad label applied to fictional works that emphasize the relationship between human

3. Mohamed Makhzangi, *Funduq al-Thaʿālib: 33 Ḥikāya ʿan al-ṭabīʿa wa-l-kāʾināt* (Cairo: Dār al-Shurūq, 2010).

societies and the natural world around them, often
with a view to questioning or displacing a tradition-
ally anthropocentric view of the world.[4] The term
ecofiction has often been associated with contemporary English-language fiction that contains overt
environmental themes, such as Edward Abbey's celebrated 1975 novel *The Monkey Wrench Gang*, or
J. M. Coetzee's *The Lives of Animals*, a philosoph-
ical argument in fictional form.[5] The term can also
be applied to those works of fiction, like *Animals in
Our Days*, that are concerned with tracing the numi-
nous, almost supernatural, connections between our
species and others. Other examples of this kind of an-
imal-focused ecofiction include Barbara Kingsolver's
novel *Flight Behavior* and Haruki Murakami's story
"The Elephant Vanishes."[6]

4. Jonathan Levin, "Contemporary Ecofiction," in *The
Cambridge History of the American Novel*, ed. Leonard Cassuto (Cambridge: Cambridge Univ. Press, 2011), 1122–36.

5. Edward Abbey, *The Monkey Wrench Gang* (New York:
HarperCollins, 2006); J. M. Coetzee, *The Lives of Animals*
(Princeton, NJ: Princeton Univ. Press, 2016).

6. Barbara Kingsolver, *Flight Behavior* (New York: Harper,
2012); Haruki Murakami, *The Elephant Vanishes: Stories*,
trans. Alfred Birnbaum and Jay Rubin (New York: Alfred A.
Knopf, 1993). Contemporary scholarly studies have also been
critical of an anthropocentric approach to social sciences. For
example, in his study of "technopolitics" and the development
of the Egyptian state, political theorist Timothy Mitchell consid-
ers the blind spots of social theory in accounting for nonhuman

Contemporary authors from the Arab world have also turned to animals in their fiction, often with the aim—like Makhzangi—of highlighting the corruption and cruelty of human society. The Libyan novelist Ibrahim al-Koni, for example, frequently contrasts the natural world of the Sahara with the menace of modern life, at times employing magical realism (one character in his novel *Nazīf al-Ḥajar* [published in English as *The Bleeding of the Stone*] transforms into a Barbary sheep to escape being conscripted into the occupying Italian army.)[7] Similarly, in the 2016 novel *al-Sabīliyyāt* (published in English as *The Old Woman and the River*) by the Kuwaiti novelist Ismāʿīl Fahd Ismāʿīl, the protagonist has a closer emotional relationship with her donkey than with other humans in the novel, including her own family members. Muhammad Afifi's fictionalized memoir *Tarānīm fī Ẓill Tamārā*, posthumously published in 1984, also places the nonhuman natural world as its emotional center,

---

agency, in particular when he examines the impact of the *Anopheles gambiae* mosquito and the deadly malaria strain it introduced to Egypt in 1942. See Timothy Mitchell, "Can the Mosquito Speak?" in *Rule of Experts: Egypt, Technopolitics, Modernity* (Berkeley: Univ. of California Press, 2002), 27–51.

7. Other modern Libyan authors have also used animals in their fiction, frequently in narratives offering an allegorical protest against political oppression. See Charis Olszok, *The Libyan Novel: Humans, Animals and the Poetics of Vulnerability* (Edinburgh: Edinburgh Univ. Press, 2020).

as the narrator affectionately observes the lives of the animals and trees that inhabit the garden behind his house.

But if animal-centered ecofiction is a fairly new development in contemporary Arabic fiction, animals themselves have a long history in Arabic's written heritage, a link that Makhzangi makes clear to his readers through the epigraphs he chooses for each story in the collection. Through these epigraphs, he points his readers to a rich tradition of writings on animals from premodern Arabic, such as the wide-ranging anthology *Kitāb al-Ḥayawān* (The Book of Animals) by al-Jāḥiẓ (d. 868 CE), the *'Ajā'ib al-Makhlūqāt* (The Wonders of Creation) by the Persian cosmographer al-Qazwīnī (d. 1283 CE), and the zoological encyclopedia *Ḥayāt al-Ḥayawān al-Kubrā* (Major Compendium on the Lives of Animals) by the Egyptian scholar al-Damīrī (d. 1405 CE).

In addition to serving as the object of study by writers examining and explicating the natural world, animals also appeared in early Arabic literary texts as speaking characters: one example would be Ibn al-Muqaffaʿ's Arabic adaptation of *Kalīla wa Dimna*, a much-translated work originally from India in the "mirrors for princes" genre, which offered moral lessons couched in the form of stories, ostensibly written to instruct rulers on how to be wise, generous, and effective. The prevalence of animals in premodern Arabic writings also reflects their prominent place in Islam. As the scholar Annemarie Schimmel has pointed out:

> Animals form an important part of Islamic tradition: they are mentioned in the Qur'an far more frequently than they are in the Bible, and all of them can serve as symbols for a spiritual truth and as warnings or admonitions for those who understand.[8]

In contrast to this literary and religious past, in which animals were held in high regard, and even taken as symbols of the human soul, Makhzangi posits a modern world characterized by heartless authoritarianism and a disconnect from the natural world. When humans fight each other, Makhzangi suggests, it is inevitably animals that suffer. As an indictment of *Homo sapiens, Animals in Our Days* offers a modern counterpart to the narrative known as "The Case of the Animals against Mankind before the King of the Jinn" from the tenth-century CE theological text *Rasā'il ikhwān al-ṣafā'* (The Epistles of the Brethren of Purity), in which animals plead their case of ill-treatment at the hands of humans in

8. Annemarie Schimmel, *Islam and the Wonders of Creation: Animal Life* (London: al-Furqan Islamic Heritage Foundation, 2003), 56. See also Sarra Tlili, *Animals in the Qur'an* (Cambridge: Cambridge Univ. Press, 2012).

a lawsuit, with the king of the jinn acting as judge.[9] In Makhzangi's stories, however, animals are not anthropomorphized. Instead, they offer silent witness to human actions, both good and bad, while opening to humans a window into a stranger and sometimes kindlier world.

In addition to an epigraph taken from a premodern Arabic text, most of the stories in the collection also open with an excerpt from a recent work of scientific journalism, highlighting current research on that animal's behavior or emotional life. By juxtaposing these epigraphs, Makhzangi seems to be drawing links between the Arabic past and modern science's understanding of animal behavior and psychology, a focus that reflects his own professional background. In a public panel in 2018, Makhzangi stated that his work in both fiction and journalism grew out of his interest in science, which remains his "greatest passion."[10] His writing career suggests a harmonious marriage of C. P. Snow's famous "two cultures" of

9. The animals make a very effective case against humanity, but ultimately the text concludes by justifying humans' dominion over the animal world. This narrative was adapted into English by Denys Johnson-Davies as a children's book with illustrations. See Denys Johnson-Davies, *The Island of Animals* (London: Quartet Books, 1994).

10. Shaymā' Shinnāwī, "Uslūb al-sard al-ʿilmī. nadwa li-l-Makhzanjī fī majmaʿ al-lugha al-ʿarabiyya," *Al-Shurūq*, November 25, 2018, https://www.shorouknews.com/news/view.aspx?cdate=25112018&id=87a6227c-e1fc-4e5a-8afd-72edb06bf2b1.

science and the arts, and Makhzangi has spoken about his optimism about the "third culture" antici-pated by Snow, one that merges an appreciation and understanding of both arts and sciences.

Makhzangi's curiosity about and sensitivity to animal life parallels his interest in other cultures and regions of the world: unsurprisingly, his stories are wide-ranging in their geographical settings. Some stories are drawn from his own extensive travels in Asia and Africa, such as "Little Purple Fish," about a visit to Ho Chi Minh's former home in Hanoi, or "On an Elephant's Back" and "White Bears/Black Bears," both narrated by a traveler in India. Some stories reflect international events and American im-perialism, beginning with the trio of opening sto-ries—"Deer," "Foal," and "Puppies"—all of which are set in the immediate aftermath of the US invasion of Iraq in 2003. Others directly touch on historical events (such as the American war in Vietnam) or are otherwise recognizably tied to real-world locations and specific histories: "The Sadness of Horses," for example, seems to be about Egypt's Tiran Island in the Red Sea, which was occupied by Israel between 1967 and 1982 and was heavily mined. "Mules" is even more oblique about its setting: the description of the two bordering countries suggests Turkey and Iraqi Kurdistan after the 1991 Gulf War, when Iraq was subject to international sanctions, but its tale of smuggling, secret orders, and impersonal violence has universal resonances.

A standout in the collection is "Enchanted Rabbits," which combines in one story almost all the themes that preoccupy Makhzangi, from humans' wanton destructiveness to the supernatural qualities of animals that can surprise or confound. In recalling his role in a nearly forgotten political uprising from his university days, the narrator describes the stark differences between the city square of twenty-six years ago and its current state, now surrounded by lofty new architecture, in place of the working-class quarters that were bulldozed long ago. The ghostly white rabbits, however, suggest a past that cannot entirely be suppressed, a marginalized counterhistory that stubbornly returns. While the mass uprising is portrayed as cathartic and politically justified, Makhzangi does not paint the mob in an entirely positive light—the righteous protest quickly turns to chaos, as looters swing from chandeliers and protesters snatch up the helpless rabbits to eat. No matter which side of the political divide humans land on—whether policemen swinging nightsticks or hungry protestors—the rabbits suffer.

The phantom rabbits that bring the narrator back to the city square, however, remain beyond human control, and indeed, beyond the realm of the explicable. They are just one example of the elements of the uncanny and the magical that Makhzangi includes in his fiction. Similarly, the metamorphosis at the heart of "The Elephants Go to Drink" and the ghostly gazelles hovering at the edge of "The Sadness of Horses" give the reader glimpses of an animal world that exists beyond our rational framework. Youssef Rakha referred to this as Makhzangi's interest in "the relation between the seen and the unseen," an interest perhaps unsurprising in an author whose writing suggests a curiosity about what lies beyond the limits of human knowledge.[11]

Other Arab authors have explored in their fiction the tension between modernity and tradition. In these stories, Mohamed Makhzangi approaches this tension from a slightly different angle, in which animals illustrate not only the negative impact of modernity, but of humanity itself. By unleashing the potent forces of mechanized warfare, unfettered capitalism, and powerful technology, modernity has not so much introduced a new amorality into the world as empowered a distinctly human tendency toward brutality. Despite this grim outlook, these stories offer moments of astonishment and grace, and encounters with animals provide "a small space for wonder" (to borrow the title of another of Makhzangi's books). If humans have an innate tendency toward oppressive behavior, Makhzangi suggests, it is animals that can reawaken our dormant capacity for awe and humility.

11. Youssef Rakha, "El-Makhzangi's Mind Games," *al-Ahram Weekly*, January 16–22, 2003.

Works Cited

Abbey, Edward. *The Monkey Wrench Gang*. New York: HarperCollins, 2006.

Abdalla, Ahmed. *The Student Movement and National Politics in Egypt: 1923–1973*. London: Saqi Books, 1985.

Afifi, Muhammad. *Little Songs in the Shade of Tamaara*. Translated by Lisa J. White. Fayetteville: Univ. of Arkansas Press, 2000.

———. *Tarānīm fī Ẓill Tamārā*. Cairo: Dar al-Shurūq, 1984.

Coetzee, J. M. *The Lives of Animals*. Princeton, NJ: Princeton Univ. Press, 1999.

al-Damīrī, Muḥammad ibn Mūsā. *Ḥayāt al-Ḥayawān al-Kubrā* [Major Compendium on the Lives of Animals]. Edited by Ibrāhīm Ṣāliḥ. Damascus: Dār al-Bashā'ir, 2005.

Ibn al-Muqaffaʻ. *Kalīla wa Dimna: akmal al-nusakh wa aṣaḥḥuhā wa aqdamuhā*. Edited by ʻAbd al-Wahhāb ʻAzzām. Beirut: Dar al-Shurūq, 2007.

Ikhwān al-Ṣafāʼ. *Rasāʼil ikhwān al-ṣafāʼ wa khullān al-wafāʼ* [The Epistles of the Brethren of Purity] 4 vols. Beirut: Dār Bayrūt, 1983.

Ismāʻīl, Ismāʻīl Fahd. *al-Sabiliyyāt*. Kuwait: Nūvā Blus li-l-nashr wa-l-tawzīʻ, 2016. Translated by Sophia Vasalou as *The Old Woman and the River* (Northampton, MA: Interlink Books, 2019).

———. *The Old Woman and the River*. Translated by Sophia Vasalou. Northampton, MA: Interlink Books, 2019.

al-Jāḥiẓ. *Kitāb al-Ḥayawān* [The Book of Animals]. Edited by ʻAbd al-Salām Hārūn. 7 vols. Cairo: Maktabat Muṣṭafā al-Bābī al-Ḥalabī wa Awlāduhu, 1938–1958.

Johnson-Davies, Denys. *The Island of Animals*. London: Quartet Books, 1994.

Kingsolver, Barbara. *Flight Behavior*. New York: Harper-Collins, 2012.

al-Kawnī, Ibrāhīm [al-Koni, Ibrahim.] *Nazīf al-Ḥajar*. Beirut: Dar al-Tanwir, 1992. Translated as *The Bleeding of the Stone* by May Jayyusi and Christopher Tingley. Northampton, MA: Interlink Books, 2002.

———. *The Bleeding of the Stone*. Translated by May Jayyusi and Christopher Tingley. Northampton, MA: Interlink Books, 2002.

Levin, Jonathan. "Contemporary Ecofiction." In *The Cambridge History of the American Novel*, edited by Leonard Cassuto, 1122–36. Cambridge: Cambridge Univ. Press, 2011.

Makhzangi, Mohamed. *Funduq al-Thaʻālib: 33 Ḥikāya ʻan al-ṭabīʻa wa-l-kāʼināt*. Cairo: Dār al-Shurūq, 2010.

———. *Ḥayawanāt Ayyāmnā*. Cairo: Dār al-Shurūq, 2006.

———. *Laḥẓāt gharaq jazīrat al-ḥūt*. Cairo: Dār al-Shurūq, 1998.

———. *Memories of a Meltdown*. Translated by Samah Selim. Cairo: American Univ. in Cairo Press, 2006.

———. *Misāḥa ṣaghīra li-l-dahsha: tajriba fī l-maqāl al-qiṣaṣī*. Cairo: Markaz al-Ahrām li-l-nashr, 2015.

Mitchell, Timothy. *Rule of Experts: Egypt, Technopolitics, Modernity*. Berkeley: Univ. of California Press, 2002.

Murakami, Haruki. *The Elephant Vanishes: Stories*. Translated by Alfred Birnbaum and Jay Rubin. New York: Alfred A. Knopf, 1993.

Olszok, Charis. *The Libyan Novel: Humans, Animals and the Poetics of Vulnerability*. Edinburgh: Edinburgh Univ. Press, 2020.

al-Qazwīnī, Zakariyyā ibn Muḥammad. *ʿAjāʾib al-makhlūqāt wa-gharāʾib al-mawjūdāt* [The Wonders of Creation and the Curiosities of the Existing World]. Edited by Fārūq Saʿd. Beirut: Dār al- Āfāq al-Jadīda, 1973.

Salih, Arwa. *The Stillborn: Notebooks of a Woman from the Student-Movement Generation in Egypt*. Translated by Samah Selim. London: Seagull Books, 2018.

Schimmel, Annemarie. *Islam and the Wonders of Creation: Animal Life*. London: al-Furqan Islamic Heritage Foundation, 2003.

Snow, C. P. *The Two Cultures and the Scientific Revolution*. Cambridge: Cambridge Univ. Press, 2012 [1959.]

Tlili, Sarra. *Animals in the Qurʾan*. Cambridge: Cambridge Univ. Press, 2012.

Animals in Our Days

Two Insights

I think you are one of those people who consider the peacock more precious to God than the crow, the pheasant dearer to Him than the kite, and the gazelle more beloved by Him than the wolf. In fact, God has differentiated these species in people's eyes, and He has made them distinct in the minds of His servants, causing some animals to be closer to mankind in appearance. He has made some domesticated, and others wild; He has made some herbivores, and others carnivores. And the same goes for the pearl, the bead, the fruit, and the pebble. So do not go by what is apparent to the eye, but follow what your mind reveals to you.

Perhaps you didn't know that man has been called the microcosm—the universe in miniature? For in him are found all the forms that are in the macrocosm. In the former we find the five senses, and in the latter the five sensibles. He is known to eat both meat and grain, a combination of what both herd animals and beasts of prey subsist on. In him can be found the eagerness of the camel, the aggression of the lion, the treachery of the wolf, the cunning of the fox, the timidity

of the nightingale, the social nature of the
ant, the industriousness of the termite, the
liberality of the rooster, the companionability
of the dog, and the unswerving direction of
the homing pigeon. Sometimes he possesses
the attributes of two or three creatures, both
herd animals and predators, at once. Yet he
cannot be a camel just because he possesses
within him the camel's sense of direction, its
jealous pride, its aggression, its rancor, and
its endurance in carrying heavy loads. Nor
does he necessarily resemble the wolf just
because he has a tendency toward a similar
treacherousness, wiliness, sense of smell,
ferocity, and intense cunning.

    —al-Jahiz, *The Book of Animals*

Deer

The eyes of the oryx between Rusafa and Jisr
    Have kindled a passion whose origin I
both know and know not.
        —Ali ibn al-Jahm

In field research, Dr. Larissa Conradt and
Professor Tim Roper discovered that the
only democratic society—amidst a sea of
authoritarian animal groups—are herds of
red deer. This was made clear to the two
researchers through the use of a computer
model to compare decision-making methods
that determined the behavior of different
groups of wild animals, and their effects on
individual animals. This unique democratic
group moves out of its grazing area only
after 62% of the deer have raised their head
from the grass once they've had enough to
eat. Similarly, when this species of deer finds
another group grazing in a particular location, it will calmly and peaceably look for
somewhere else to graze. The deer collec-
tively agree on taking these peaceful democratic decisions through special agreed-upon
signals, via body language among members
of the group.
        —*Focus Science Magazine*

The marines entered the palace after a long night full of the lightning of explosions and the thunder of bombardments, the noise of destruction and the crackling of flames. They entered with the first rays of a dawn weighed down by thick smoke and the smell of burning corpses. They were exhausted and hungry, but drunk on a victory they had never imagined they would achieve so quickly. It only exacerbated their feeling of hunger and drove them to comb through the presidential palace and gardens in search of something to eat. That's where they found the deer, and the lions, too.

The deer were paralyzed with terror, hugging the hedges that ran along the walkways of the palace gardens. The marines had no difficulty catching them and dragging them over to where they were celebrating in the president's reception hall, where a fire pit for grilling had been lit using wood from chairs hand-carved by the world's most skilled furniture makers and covered in layers of pure French gold leaf. Other marines discovered the lions while searching the rest of the palace. Four lions in gleaming rust-free steel cages. They were hungry, growling and pacing back and forth in their cages, their throats wracked by hunger, smoke, and dust. The lions belonged to the president's son, and the rumor was that when he was angry with someone, he would feed them to the lions. Some of the marines proposed setting aside some of the deer meat so they could amuse themselves by feeding the lions after their own feast was over.

The suggestion got lost amid the victors' noisy clamor, and the scent of the brazen grilling of the meat of twenty plump white Arabic oryx and ten marvelous desert gazelles that looked as though they had been created from a gentle breeze adorned with flower buds. By the time the sun had fully risen, all those deer had become charred white bones, flecked with a few bits of cooked flesh. After they had had their fill, many of the marines dozed off where they were sitting, on comfortable chairs. Others stayed awake and brought bones to the lions' cages, unaware that lions won't touch cooked meat. Would lions deign to lick charred, leftover bones?

Foal

A wise man was asked: "What possession is the most noble?" He replied: "A horse, followed by another horse, which has in its belly a third horse."

—al-Damiri, *Major Compendium on the Lives of Animals*

Trembling, the small foal scurried between his mother's legs when the sound of explosions struck his ears and the lightning flash of bombs glimmered in his eyes. He couldn't hear the voices of any of the humans he was familiar with, not even the terrifying voice of the president's son, whose arrival at the palace race track instantly caused the grooms to tremble and made the horses quake. His voice was rough, and his hand heavy and brutal. He had big teeth that showed when he scowled at other people or laughed with the foal—for him alone the president's son laughed. He would place his right hand around the foal's neck and burst out laughing while taking some sugar out of his pocket for him, the purest kind of sugar in the world. He would feed it to him with affection and delight, but he was harsh and irritable toward everyone else. Once the foal saw him beating a stable hand who was slow to saddle his horse. After the stable hand fell to the ground, the president's son kicked him with the iron spurs of his riding boot, and kept kicking his head until blood poured out of his nose, mouth, and ears. He gave the foal's own mother a hard slap when she shied away a little just as he was about to ride. He kept slapping her on the muzzle while she bucked, whinnying pitifully, until blood poured from her jaws. He didn't stop hitting her until the foal ran up and came between him and his mother.

The foal felt the tension in his mother's warm stomach above him. She was stifling the restless movement in her legs so as not to bump against the body of her little one taking shelter up against her. She stood in place and trembled whenever bombs reverberated or the flash of explosions lit up the sky. During the few lulls, no sooner did she relax and he could feel the warm flow of her affection, than the noise and flashes would start up again. Deafening noise, then silence. Deafening noise, then silence. Fires, the sound of buildings collapsing, and screams. Then after a long grueling night, a terrible silence prevailed. With the first light of dawn, the foal heard a clamor of human voices shouting at each other, and hurrying footsteps, then a lot of people burst in on them, their faces covered in dust and their eyes red. They started fighting with each other around the fenced corral. Then the gate was thrown open, and the foal could feel his mother's body trying to get away from the rough rope around her neck. Another piece of rope went around his neck, too, and he saw himself running with his mother, bound together to a rope tied to the back of a ramshackle pickup truck that clattered down long rubble-filled streets. Fires blazed on either side of them. Corpses were scattered about. Chaos reigned.

The foal wanted to nestle close to his mother, so he picked up his pace, but when he got up beside her, he found her with her neck pulled tight by the lasso that bound her behind the fast-moving pickup. She couldn't turn her head to him, but he saw her constricted eyes go white, sending tormented glances in his direction. He neighed as he ran up beside her, and she neighed back in response, a choked-off whinny coming out of a throat that was fighting off suffocation. The neighing stopped abruptly, and he no longer heard anything but the sound of desperate gasping and the clatter of metal. He increased his speed, and got up between his mother's legs, but she stumbled, and her large warm body fell on top of him. He was crushed between the warmth of her stomach and the asphalt of the road. He heard her ragged breaths, and saw her legs, scraped over the dusty asphalt, trembling, bleeding, trembling.

Puppies

The dog: He has no peace of mind; because
his condition is one where he can expect
misery, anticipating one tribulation after
another. If he isn't safe and sound, no
creature suffers more than he does. If he
has been trained to be obedient while he is
still a puppy, then even if there is meat on
the butcher's block, he won't sniff it, and he
won't even go near it. Yet of all God's cre-
ations, he has the best sense of smell.

—al-Jahiz, *The Book of Animals*

On the eve of the annual flooding of the Nile,
a bright star usually appears in the sky. It
gives a warning, as it were, of the impending
flood. Unable to account for the appearance
of the star in a rational way, the Egyptians
saw it as a manifestation of the supernatural. They associated in their minds with a
dog that barks to warn of the approach of
a stranger. So the star was named Sirius (a
hound), and the dog itself became a sacred
embodiment of watchfulness. Its represen-
tations appeared above the doorways in the
temple of Osiris and Isis, and subsequently
on other temples as well.

—Yuri Dmitriyev, *Man and Animals*

The bombing had stopped the day before, and people emerged onto the street in the light of day. Lingering fires were still smoking, and rubble from collapsed buildings was scattered everywhere. Columns of tanks and armored cars made their way through the streets and spread out into the city squares. The invaders fully occupied the city, and with that, these same invaders brought down the regime that had ruled oppressively for thirty-five years. In the burned-out city, people didn't welcome them with flowers, but they did rush out amid the ruins with the lighthearted step of people who had escaped a lifetime of surveillance: they were liberated but apprehensive. A mood of escape and exhaustion hung over everything, even over the neglected animals scattered everywhere. Most of them were stray dogs with small puppies trailing behind. There were a lot of them, with their own enigmatic look about them, in the large public garden by the riverbank where dozens of people had gathered, squatting on their haunches, leaning down, stretching themselves flat on the ground, and getting grass and dirt in their ears, as if to listen closely to the voices of those who had gone missing. It was rumored that their voices were seeping out of secret prisons underground. Voices of brothers, friends, relatives, loved ones, neighbors and acquaintances— dozens, hundreds, thousands of them—who had disappeared years ago in the dark recesses of the regime that had been toppled the day before. The story went around that the regime had thrown them into massive underground prisons, and there was a rumor that they had learned of the regime's downfall when they saw their guards flee, leaving the ironclad doors shut behind them, and that they had begun calling for help, shouting for someone to release them. There were some who swore they had heard their cries. Some tried to make out these voices by placing their ears on the ground and not talking, except in whispers or with hand gestures. A strange silence prevailed over the whole garden. The dogs responded to it by standing still themselves and listening, using their sense of hearing that can pick up things that human ears can't. Their ears perked up, and they bent low, their heads bowed down at an angle to better pick up sounds. They seemed confused, unable to tell whether the muffled rumbling coming from within the earth was the voices of those shackled in deeply buried prisons, or a muted echo of the caterpillar tracks on an invader's armored car that was now crushing asphalt, the remnants of burnt, shattered palm trees, and the bones of the killed and injured scattered in the streets. As for the puppies, whose young sense of hearing was extremely sharp, and who could hear what neither the older dogs nor humans could, they experienced a strange, intense trembling, and let out pitiful sounds like lamentations.

Brass Grasshoppers

The grasshopper: a kind of locust that chirps, hops and flies.

—Abridged Dictionary

The cricket (also called the grasshopper): also known as the "night chirper" as al-Jawhari called it. It is a hopping insect that resembles a locust. Al-Maidani has said: *The cricket is a species of beetle that makes a noise in desert regions from the early evening to morning. When someone looks for it, they don't see it, and therefore they have coined the phrase "more hidden than a cricket."*

—al-Damiri, Major Compendium on the Lives of Animals

On the right side of Sukhumvit Street, if you're heading toward Phuket Road and Siam Square, is one of the largest and most extensive markets of knock-off goods in the world. The "fake vendors" spread their wares on folding tables that run the length of the sidewalk for several kilometers, haphazardly arranged under dingy umbrellas. All their wares are fakes and knock-offs: purses, clothes, watches, sandals, tableware, paintings, wood carvings, perfumes, butchers' knives, lamps, countless things that carry international name brands—all of them counterfeits. Also there were the brass grasshoppers I bought.

I wasn't satisfied with buying just one grasshopper. Instead, I bought—for a quarter of the price the seller was asking—two grasshoppers in small paper containers lined with cloth and covered with elegant Chinese lettering. When I was looking them over in front of the seller, I was unable to get a quick look at the hidden device that made them chirp. The chirp made by this "toy" (they were sold as toys) matched the chirping of real grasshoppers.

I had discovered what was different about them as I hurried along the stinking passageway between the tables of counterfeit-goods vendors and the small sidewalk restaurants selling strange foods: smoked, almost embalmed, duck meat; fish sliced and dried like mummies; boiled eggs whose white flesh, by some obscure method of preparation, had turned a bright black color. And unbearable smells that always made me hurry past this place whenever I was in Bangkok. But this time I was forced to slow down, when chirping caught my attention in the middle of this bright Asian daylight.

Grasshoppers chirping in broad daylight? I asked myself in astonishment as I hurried along. I slowed down when I realized that the chirping was coming from the sidewalk vendors' tables. I stopped and went up to them, leaning over one of the tables where dozens of small paper containers were lined up. The sound grew louder as I got closer. I heard the seller shouting on the other side: "One hundred baht each! One hundred baht!" I thought it was likely that the small paper containers were the source of the chirping; I was certain of it when I saw brass grasshoppers vibrating in some open boxes, gleaming against the backdrop of the boxes' red satin lining. The grasshoppers were metallic and bright. There was one in each box, and each one started chirping when the wrapping was opened and stopped when the box closed! I started opening and shutting boxes and looking into others that had the same brass grasshoppers in them—and the same thing happened each time. It was a marvelous toy, and I bought two of them. I decided I would start figuring out the secret of their chirping as soon as I got back to the hotel.

The Greece Hotel, which is where I usually stayed whenever I spent time in Bangkok, was an amazing human circus: entertaining, and so cheap it was hard to put much faith in its five-star rating. Arabic newspapers were regularly available there, since it was located in Nana Plaza, which was crowded with Arabs and Arabic restaurants. It was also a few steps away from Sukhumvit Street, the street I simultaneously despised and couldn't stay away from. It was a gathering place for repulsive things, oddities, and attractions, as well as all the services a traveler could ask for: airline offices, currency exchange places, several gigantic business centers, and three of the best book-stores in the world.

In the basement floors beneath the hotel lobby there were a number of gambling halls, nightclubs, saunas, and massage parlors, and the most incredible display room I saw in all the countries I ever visited or passed through. They say it opened during the Vietnam War, to cater to the lust of marines on leave in Thailand. It was a room that displayed prostitutes crowded together on a revolving platform draped in dark red velvet, behind a glass partition that surrounded the platform and formed a display window that a customer would stand in front of so he could pick out which one of the half-naked revolving girls he wanted, while they went all out in displaying their charms, gesturing that they were looking for a "date" and blowing kisses. In the lobby, the main rooms, the hallways, and the other floors and rooms, all the worldly pleasures intermingled freely, protected by a veil of secrecy, even if it was invisible. It was an enormous establishment for dealing and doing drugs, drinking, whoring, gambling, smuggling gems and rare sandalwood, for shady money-laundering deals, for licenses to export counterfeit goods. It was a giant brothel and a den of thieves where violent crimes took place. In the depths of night there were endless drunken brawls; everywhere you could hear Arabic, Turkish, and Urdu spoken. It seemed that the place also attracted Westerners, who, like the Middle Eastern guests at the hotel, took to speaking in loud voices and with constant hand gestures. Perhaps it was this hubbub that allowed me to enter without anyone noticing. One of the grasshoppers burst out in forceful and insistent chirping, which made me pick up my pace, thinking that the box's cover must have opened up.

My curiosity was piqued, so as soon as I entered my room I began looking for the secret behind the brass grasshoppers' chirping. I picked up one of the boxes. I opened it, and the chirping started up. I closed it and it stopped. I covered the open box with my hand and the sound stopped. When I took my hand away, it started up again. I eagerly began examining its inner workings. I wasn't keen on discovering the secret of the grasshopper's vibrations, since it seemed straightforward to me: it was a reaction to the box's movement via tension in a small spring that must have been planted inside it. But I was stumped about how to explain the sound it made. Because the sound repeatedly cut off when I covered the box with my palm, and started up again when I removed my hand, I thought it likely that the sound was triggered by light. So I started feeling around for a photoelectric cell, which would be hidden under the satin or perhaps between the layers of paper of the box itself. The box was quite beautiful and I didn't dare tear it: I was satisfied with the explanation I had reached. Before I turned off the light and went to sleep, I noticed that the words HANDMADE IN CHIANG RAI were written on the bottom of the box.

Chiang Rai—which I had once passed through when I was traveling around northern Thailand—was a dubious city, inasmuch as it was considered the gateway to the Golden Triangle, which encompasses the border region between Laos, Burma, and Thailand. It was once considered the capital of East Asia's opium and heroin trade, before it was forced to switch to growing plants and flowers and light manufacturing. Perhaps it was thinking about Chiang Rai before I fell asleep that made me dream that I was fleeing mysterious pursuers in a wide field covered with fluttering red and white poppy blossoms. Then the poppy stalks turned into rusty steel bars that surrounded me, blocking my escape. They made a continual clanking noise while I tried desperately to squeeze through them. At the same time, a feeling that I couldn't breathe welled up inside me, and I experienced an intense sensation of suffocating. Then I woke up.

The room was dark. There were furious knocks on the door that separated my room from the neighboring one, but it didn't instantly cause me alarm, as it should have. There was something that reassured me a bit: since I usually get nervous about a door like that, I make sure to lock it completely before going to sleep. In fact, I take the precaution of putting a table behind it, weighing it down with the heaviest bags it can support. Then I prop it up with all the chairs, sofas, and bedside tables I can drag over to it. That's what I had done the day before. The person in the next room was a Turkish man shouting curses at me with ugly language, only some of which I understood. In the moment of silence between his banging on the door and his insults, I could hear the sounds of the grasshoppers' chirping. I was amazed by this unexpected burst of chirping in the darkened room.

I turned on all the lights in the room and went to look for my boxes of brass grasshoppers. I could only find one, and I began racking my brains trying to remember where I had left the other one, which I had been examining before going to sleep. Where had it gone? There are only a finite number of objects in hotel rooms and it's impossible to lose a brightly colored box like that. I searched, but I couldn't find anything. The chirping had turned into a shrill, grating noise that made it impossible to sleep. It made the Turkish man's outbursts and insults coming through the locked door seem tolerable by comparison. Then I became aware of another racket coming from the hallway outside.

I opened the door of my room a crack so I could peek out, and instantly retreated in fear: most of the occupants of the neighboring rooms were outside their doors in their nightclothes, shouting insults at each other in a Babel of languages and shaking their fists, while behind them, through the slightly ajar doors, I could see prostitutes. They were caught up in the excitement, sticking their heads, necks, shoulders, and a little of their bare chests out in the hallway.

I realized the danger I was up against, since nothing is more foul-tempered than angry drunks when their wild revelries have been interrupted. It must have been the grasshoppers' chirping that annoyed my neighbor and disrupted his pleasant state of intoxication. It had riled him up, and his furious banging and shouting irritated the others, who in turn had been stirred up further.

The wee hours of the night were lit up with this uproar, and I hurried to wedge the bed behind the main door of the room, fearing that one of the drunks might open it. But the order to surrender reached me from inside the room: the hotel management had sent several hotel staff to my room: one of the angry men, or housekeeping, or the floor supervisors must have called the front desk. When they knocked on the door and I didn't open, they called the hotel management, who then called me. The person on the phone said I was violating the rules for hotel guests by bothering my neighbors. I told him I wasn't bothering anyone— he could come and see for himself. He asked me to open the door for the hotel staff so they could confirm that. No sooner had I opened the door a crack than I was surprised by an onslaught of drunken men trying to force their way in, along with the hotel staff. I quickly slammed the door shut, and made sure to lock it from inside. Then I sat down, surrounded by nearby chirping and distant shouting. Nervously, I thought about which objects I could use to defend myself with if they attacked me. I thought I might need to leave the hotel to look for somewhere safe.

I didn't wait for the hotel management to call me again, but took the initiative to call them, saying that angry drunks were threatening to murder me, and that I would only leave my room with police protection. I assumed that the arrival of the police in their official uniforms would prevent the angry men from making any sudden hostile moves. I gathered up my things from the room and packed my suitcase. I put on my outdoor clothes, and as I waited for the police to arrive, the only thing I heard—despite the unceasing clamor around me—was the chirping of the lost grasshopper that I was still furiously looking for.

I pulled the paintings off the wall, tossed the chairs into a corner of the room, flipped the mattress off the bed, pulled the drawers out of the desk, and nearly ripped the closet doors off their bottom railing when I opened them, but in the whole room, there was only the one grasshopper in the closed box. At 2:00 a.m., three policemen came to accompany me to another hotel. I didn't forget to put the closed box with the grasshopper in it in my shirt pocket as I left.

They found me a room at a hotel close to the ones on Sukhumvit Street. It was called the Ambassador, a large old-fashioned hotel surrounded by gardens of winding plants of luxuriant green, continuously lit from above by powerful lamps that mimicked daylight, which turned on automatically once the sunlight was gone. I was hungry and exhausted, so much so that I preferred to stay in the lobby café, which looked out onto one of the interior gardens, so I could sip a cup of tea and eat a piece of cake. I went up to the newspaper rack in a corner of the café and pulled out a glossy English-language magazine. My attention was drawn to an illustrated feature under the title, "Chiang Rai . . . Memories of Opium!"

The article talked about the Opium Museum that had officially opened in Chiang Rai, now that growing and selling opium had been banned in the region. It was a small museum that told the story of opium growing and heroin production, drug-preparation methods and paraphernalia, and the different kinds of harm it causes people. The museum displayed all of that, along with a collection of photos, instruments, and rare acquisitions. In addition to the article on the museum, the magazine provided a history of the explosion in the drug trade in the Golden Triangle. As a border region shared by Laos, Burma, and Thailand, it underwent a noticeable economic boom when this trade flourished during the Vietnam War. But after the war ended, when the United States came to feel that the dangers posed by the drug trade were reaching its own shores and had begun to destroy the lives of America's youth, it started putting pressure to eradicate opium harvesting and selling in the region. Thailand responded favorably to that initiative, in return for assistance for its opium growers to help them make the switch to vegetable and flower farming, and to small local industries. The switch occurred, but the promised assistance never arrived, so drug operations resumed, albeit in secret. Along with this clandestine activity, a new, aboveground revenue stream was born: counterfeit goods—impressively made knock-offs of every kind, from Levis and Lee Cooper jeans to DLC bags, Swiss Army knives, Rolex and Cartier watches, Chanel perfumes, Max Factor and Christian Dior beauty products, accessories from Yves Saint Laurent, and others.

The tea and cake had arrived, so I began mechanically sipping and nibbling at them, still reading and looking at the photos. I forgot all about the tea and cake when I became absorbed in reading a full-page sidebar to a longer article titled "Legacy of the Forgotten War." At the bottom, the editors noted that it had been excerpted from a book by the American writer Joe Cummings, who, citing a nonfiction book by a British writer, Christopher Robbins, related the events of a massive covert operation launched by the CIA, code-named The Ravens. This operation continued from 1964 to 1973, and the world didn't know a thing about it. It began after the signing of the 1962 Geneva Accords between the United States and North Vietnam and went on until the decision was made to halt the terrible American bombing of Laos, in exchange for a commitment by all parties to remove any belligerent forces from Lao territory and an indemnification of Laos' losses through appropriate American assistance. US intelligence had a number of American pilots commissioned as secret agents for the

CIA, wearing civilian uniforms, so they could pilot planes for the well-known civilian airline Air America. Under cover of transporting aid and assistance, these planes began shipping opium and heroin as part of a clandestine business operation. Two million dollars flowed into the United States every day—an amount that in a single day covered all the assistance America had offered to Laos over a period of several years. The remaining profits from this business were used to cover the costs of military operations for the American army in Vietnam. The Ravens operation was so secret that its existence was only alluded to by the phrase *theater of operations on the other side.* The American pilots were CIA agents, required to carry small cyanide pills in secret pockets inside their clothes in the event that any of them was captured. Until now, the secret of this "forgotten war," as the investigation called it, had never been revealed.

Absent-mindedly, I placed the magazine on the empty seat next to me. Slowly I started sipping the tea, which had gone cold, as I gobbled up what remained of the piece of cake, which by now had lost its flavor. I was only aroused from my absent-minded state by a sensation of something moving along my neck. I ran my fingertips over my neck, and when they bumped up against something solid there, I jumped out of my chair with a yelp and immediately threw it onto the floor. It was a brass grasshopper. I found its box, open and empty, in my shirt pocket. How had the box gotten open? And how did this brass grasshopper get out? How could it have climbed onto my neck?

While some of the café's patrons gave me furtive, puzzled glances in response to my shouting, I picked up the grasshopper and placed it on the table. On the dark marble surface, I observed the sparkling grasshopper. I leaned over it as closely as I could. All of its delicate gilded legs moved whenever it felt stillness, and they stopped moving at the slightest motion that escaped from me, even from the tips of my fingers. I picked up the knife and fork and went to work; I took apart the grasshopper's golden wings and its brown-black body appeared beneath them. I separated the chest from the stomach, and its living structure was revealed as it turned and turned again in fear, with its head and half of its severed body, as specks of metal coating fell away from it, a fine brass ash that scattered over the surface of the green-veined black marble.

Pursuing a Butterfly in the Sea

Many a great one have the small disturbed . . .
and in the seas, other seas drown.
—From al-Jahiz, quoting a poet,
The Book of Animals

At the water's edge, at a time when the beach was empty of people, in the early morning toward dawn, when the sea had receded to its lowest ebb, I paused to watch the man in his wheelchair as he pushed its wheels with the remaining strength in his arms. He left two deep tracks, parallel and separate, imprinted in the wet sand. Sometimes the water filled them, and other times it left them empty. It was only a matter of minutes before the water began to rise over the wheels. The chair seemed as though it would gently sink beneath the rising tide, but something surprising swelled up from below the seat and made it float like a raft rising and falling on the water: the man had equipped his chair with an inflatable cushion. At the right moment, he pressed a button under his hand on the chair's right armrest, and it caused the chair to float. The chair bobbed on the water as he directed it where he wanted to go. It could go forward or back up, and turn right or left, so that the two wheels beneath his hands were transformed into both rudders and propellers together.

Now he is riding on the surface of the sea, but he isn't going far out from shore—rather, he is going deep into the memory of a day that he once told me about, a day fixed in a distant time, when he would go out into the sea on two living, healthy legs. He would wade into the water until it reached his chest and then come back. But that day he noticed it in the water. A surprising shudder and warmth overcame him; his conscious mind went blank as the water grew turbulent.

His hand shot out into the water to grab this radiant yellow "butterfly," but he wasn't paying attention. He wasn't paying attention to the water that had begun to rise with the return of high tide. He wasn't paying attention to his limited experience with the ocean—he who didn't dare to go down to the water unless it was at low tide. Perhaps the water's calm had enticed him, as he lingered floating on its surface, to drift aimlessly for a spell. He enjoyed observing the kingdoms of the ocean floor, above which the turquoise waters of low tide appeared clear and translucent. Perhaps he was swayed by his diver-like appearance, as he sported a face mask, a breathing tube, and a spear gun hanging from his shoulder. Perhaps that gaudily beautiful yellow had taken over his rational mind, the yellow that belonged to the butterfly fish that he clearly had never imagined existed outside of full-color films and glossy photo books about the Red Sea ocean floor.

The water was disturbed and the fish swerved away, but he didn't lose sight of it. It sped off into the distance, and his eyes followed it across the same expanse. His arms pumped through the water, and his feet struck its surface in turn. The splashing from his exertions flew high up in the air and fell down again. It struck his sun-warmed back with coolness and moisture. He was seized by the desire to possess the sea butterfly, even as it resisted him. He summoned everything he had within him at that moment and focused it on the bottleneck tail of the yellow fish in front of him: *I won't let it escape*! He struck out with his arms, and his feet felt the burn as he kicked, like the outboard of a motorboat in hot pursuit. The animal he kept shackled inside himself burst through the restraint of its chains with a defiant jolt of energy. His speed gave him a shot of euphoria, and he went faster. *I'm yours, sea butterfly, or else you're mine. No question about it—I've got you*! The snorkel began to draw water into his mouth along with air, and between drinking in the heavy salt water, the breathing, and the coughing, he got carried away with himself. Nothing except a collision would stop him. He forgot about his house on the beach that he had worked so hard to furnish, and his bride who was waiting for him there. He forgot his bed, which was the only place he found rest, forgot about people, and forgot about everything that was his or would be his as he shot out like a dart flying through a gun barrel. His arm strokes drove him to push harder, and his leg kicks spurred him on to harder kicks, as though his advance as he swam along the water's surface had been turned into a tank with treads, plowing through a terrain that was a mix of rough ground and soft spots—or soft ground and rough spots, he couldn't say. He only felt his being struggling with the water, and his arms thrusting and slapping, then plowing through and pushing as they plunged his sluggish body further along. *I'm cutting through water, I'm cutting through water*, he kept repeating giddily to himself. He didn't know, or didn't want to know: was he just fighting against the water, or was he after the sea butterfly? Whenever he focused his mind on his body, now on fire with thrusting and kicking, the world shrank down to the expanses of sea floor slipping, slipping past, and to a yellow fish fleeing before him. His mind wandered as he felt himself both the center of this commotion and its observer. But he kept going. He wished he could keep going to the utmost, but he felt something preventing him from going as fast as he'd like, and it was weighing down his right side.

He remembered the spear gun on his left shoulder. He remembered it was loaded. A dark thought flittered through his mind: he imagined the sea butterfly impaled on the spear's tip, dead: its brilliant yellow color lost as it faded to the color of mud, its scales falling off as it turned ash gray and slippery. He could feel the bitter, nauseous taste of the raw, colored fish of the Red Sea in his mouth. His swimming flagged. Just thinking about it was too much for him, and he asked himself: *What's happening? What's happening?* A moment of dark panic swept over his being. He stopped swimming and paused to float, motionless, spreading his body out on the water's surface. Then, fearful and fumbling, as though doing it for the first time, he swam using only his right side, letting his legs slowly kick the water. He raised his left shoulder out of the water and lowered his waist, turning himself over until he was half-standing in the water, so he could change direction and look toward shore. But he couldn't find it. There was no shore as far as the eye could see; no red mountain peaks looming on the horizon! He must be ten kilometers—at least— from shore. The waters of high tide had rolled in, and there was nothing there except water, water, water. Dark blue waves rose, fell, and collided with each other. His heart sank. He felt an inhuman fear, and a sense of his own smallness. He broke out into a mad burst of swimming to head back, although he wasn't convinced he was even heading in the right direction. He swam, and in an instant, the idea popped into his head that he should alternate between swimming and floating so as not to exhaust himself. But when he started floating, he found his body growing heavy. The ocean opened its gaping mouth, and the water was on the verge of swallowing him up. Terrified, he quickly started swimming again.

In a fleeting moment, he recalled the butterfly fish, and his memory of it was bound up with an emotion like shame. A desire like an impulse to burst into tears pulled at him. But he couldn't dwell on it, so long as he kept swimming like a man possessed, expending all the energy his four limbs possessed. He rested for a little while with his cheek against the water's surface and noticed the splash made by his legs, which were still kicking, as though they had a will of their own. *I will reach safety, I will reach safety*, his spirit said. Seeing his legs splashing was like a breath of fresh air for him, but it was instantly followed by the thought *Am I about to die?* He felt sorrow and grief, seeing his corpse floating on the water, tossed by a wave onto the beach along with sea spray. *Who will mourn me?* The face of his bride loomed over the water, fixed in place for a moment, then vanished like scattered mist. Then he saw his mother dressed in mourning, overwhelmed by tears and wracked by loud sobs.

The sound of the strokes of his arms and the kicking of his legs came to him in waves, alternately loud and subdued. Then he became aware of his own voice, when he found himself groaning with every arm stroke. Pain raged through his left shoulder like a knife sinking into flesh and bone. He remembered he still had the spear gun on his shoulder. *Should I throw it away?* he asked himself. He had just about stretched his right hand to his shoulder when, without warning, the air escaped from his lungs and he found himself sinking—or rather he was hurled below the water, his legs dragging his body down. It occurred to him that he should search for the bottom with his toes: perhaps he could stand on it and rest a little, but he was dismayed when he couldn't find the bottom. *Am I about to die?* Terror and a profound feeling of loneliness clung to him as he opened his eyes in the water and beheld greens and blues suffused with light. He saw luminous bubbles gush forth and rise to the surface in abundance around him. *Am I dying?* Familiar voices, and other voices that were strange to him, called out his name repeatedly, coupled with the phrase *He's dead, he's dead, he's dead.* He was astonished that he was feeling no pain, and it was only the sensation of water getting into his ears that made him shout. He realized that his body was swallowing water and wasn't breathing. He thought for sure that would drag him even more toward the bottom, since absorbing water would only make him heavier. Then his mind grew strangely clear, and he was possessed by an insight steeped in both tenderness and despair: *I'm going to die. I'm going to die.*

He began swallowing more water as he seemed to descend toward the ocean floor like a speck of dust floating down in a beam of light. He heard the sea roaring with a sound that had no echo, and with his clear mind he could hear his name repeated, coupled with *Ha, Ha, Ha!*, with a tinge of sorrow and derision. It was as though it were sending his name off on its final farewell and extending along with it into distant horizons of light-saturated water. *Ha, ha!* But no sooner had it vanished than fear blazed up in him, a horrible fear of death by drowning. He reckoned he would linger in a prolonged agony, until everything came to an end. So he burst out kicking and thrashing his arms and legs in the hope of rising to the surface. *I don't want to die by drowning.* He thrashed upward, thrashed, and thrashed again, until the sea's muffled roar broke off and he came up to the air and breathed in. He found himself swimming again without hearing or seeing—or rather, he saw and heard without understanding anything except that he was swimming. He was swimming without being sure of anything. In this deaf and blind state he was distracted by the certain knowledge that he would not die by choking on a lungful of water. Instead, he would die as quickly as possible. Anything to escape the torment of drowning.

That strange clarity of mind that had momentarily revealed itself to him underwater returned, and he could see and hear again. He saw the rowing motion of his arms and the clash of the waves; he heard the noisy splash of his legs and the garrulous ocean; he heard the echo of determination within himself: *I will die as I wish—quickly—and not by drowning against my will.*

He brought his head down, letting his feet rise up, and he was easily able to remove the spear gun from his shoulder underwater. Copious glowing green bubbles burst forth and rose up around him as he plunged his head below. His spirit was cheered by this twinkling, this green color, but it saddened just as quickly: *I don't have the energy to swim all these absurd kilometers. I will die with one shot that will make me lose consciousness, rather than suffer the dark fate of drowning.* He was thinking about aiming the muzzle of the spear gun at his head and pressing the trigger. The spear would pierce through his skull to the brain, tearing through its twisted coils, and he would feel no pain or drowning.

There was an icy coldness freezing his joints, and a pain he had never known before was pounding on his shoulders, upper arms, thighs and wrists, pinching and flaring up beyond endurance. It was driving him to think about an easy death as he sought to escape from the pain of saving himself: *I have no strength in these two arms, and there's no fight left in my legs.* He went limp, and the clarity of mind returned to him. He went back to plunging his head underwater to prepare to fire the spear gun point-blank at himself. As he sank, he felt the gun's muzzle brush his hair, and he shuddered. He hesitated to pull the trigger. He felt like he was on the verge of tears, and his spirit trembled: *Is this how I lose my life, by being driven to die by my own hand?* Currents of water were washing over him, and his whole life passed before him in a filmstrip of soundless images. He saw people he hadn't thought about in years and viewed scenes he hadn't thought still existed within himself. He wanted to laugh a little, and immediately afterward loathed the idea. He didn't know if he was crying or laughing. Then the images were compressed and constricted before his eyes and trickled to black as he spurred himself to press the trigger.

Water flashed before his eyes—white, then green, then the color red burst out of it, and bright bubbles of blood were everywhere. A twinge of pain stung his back, a sudden twinge, and suddenly he felt his thighs limp and heavy. His empty hands were striking the surface of the water. *I didn't die! Why didn't I die?!* He inhaled as he emerged to the surface, gulping the air of the living world and exhaling in shock. The spear had missed his brain but it had struck his back, piercing his spinal column and paralyzing his legs. *I'm going to die paralyzed, by drowning*! He felt regret and cruel irony as the water grew high around him. He struck out at the water with his arms. Sometimes he moved past the mix of water and his blood; sometimes the bloody water got ahead of him. He saw his life poured out in red, and in the interstices between grief and numbness he noticed smooth circular surfaces approaching him. He noticed dark masses dart out in a sliding motion beneath these circles. He saw a piercing gimlet eye and a jaw inscribed with teeth. He found himself punching into the water with his arms, and only his arms.

He was dragging his dead legs and felt the spear still lodged between his vertebrae, spreading pain and numbness in his bones. He was like a man possessed, or one driven insane. He swam far from the warning sign of black fins sticking out over the water's surface. *Sharks are attracted by the smell of blood, the color of blood*: the idea flashed into his brain, and without turning he could see the sharks' greedy mouths. He saw unblinking eyes and rows of sharp triangular teeth looking over his flesh. He heard a chirping and squeaking. He heard sounds like rusty joints moving, and he swam furiously to escape from a jaw about to snap at him from behind at any moment. Again he heard a sound like whistling, and a bird flew by, startling him as it soared away over his head. He turned sideways somehow—and it came to him, in spite of all this bitter paralysis and fear. He saw it but didn't understand. He saw the smooth circular shapes following him and he saw their eyes. He was astonished to find, between their eyes, fountains shimmering in the light. Clouds of thick spray rose straight up in the air, then scattered like silver-misted volleys spread out behind him. He was fleeing straight ahead while feelings of wonder came in flashes, ricocheting off each other inside him. *How can I . . . ? How could I . . . ?* It was an instant of madness, no doubt, that moment when the shore spread out at the edge of his vision. He saw Mount Abu Dukhan draw near, undulating on the horizon in gray, blue, red, yellow, and pink. And beneath it, he beheld the old wooden beach cabins of Hurghada scattered about, some perched above others. Then he could see individual people shouting and calling out as they hurried toward him. One of them was on a raft and plowing through the water with a long paddle. Another waded into the surf, which barely came up to his waist, followed by two others who waded in up to their knees. *Aaaaah!* he screamed. He heard his voice as he had never heard it before. It was a primal scream of remorse coming from bottomless depths within him, followed by the sounds of chirping, squeaking, and whistling. The word *dolphins* flashed into his brain. Then he turned back, his heart bursting with emotion. He saw powerful tails thrashing high in the air, then a parade of snouts and slippery shining backs following behind him. A row of dolphins prompted by instinct to lift him up in jets of water so he wouldn't sink. He was intermittently conscious of the fact that he had been rescued: the spouts of water through the blowholes, the powerful tails, the smooth circles of water, the mountain, the seashore, the people, the raft, the paddle. *They're coming to rescue me.* He felt certain that the dolphins would carry him if swimming got to be too much for him and that people would get to him if his arms grew tired. He was astonished at how he had swum all this distance with his arms—just his arms—after injuring his legs.

He saw seagulls circling over the waters of the beach, their white bellies gleaming turquoise with the color of the water. Their cries were loud and distressing. Then he was surprised to feel his hands bumping against the sandy ocean floor. He had just enough strength to draw himself up to a sitting position in this shallow water until he could be rescued. The front of the raft grazed his forehead, and he burst into tears as he remembered his legs. The knot in his stomach relaxed, like an engine powering down when it's stopped its spinning. He went limp when he reached out and touched the edge of the boat, then fell unconscious as hands took hold of him.

And now, now, he recalls all of that, fastening his memory to the rhythm of a mysterious hour in his life. As he recalls the final moment, the moment he fainted in those arms all those years ago, he notices the water receding with the ebbing tide and notices sandbars emerging beneath him. He realizes that the wheels of the wheelchair are resting on moist sand and he sets off, tracing two deep lines in the sand. Advancing in parallel lines, they don't retrace his earlier tracks. They move off into the distance, as does he, before the sun rises and people flock to the beach.

Little Purple Fish

Most people think that fish are deaf, but they
are not . . . Fish can hear quiet sounds that
we can hardly hear, and they can usually distinguish between one tone and another . . .
Thus their tone distinction is far from being
as good as ours, and this is to be expected
since the structure of their ears is far less
complex. But the memory of the fishes for
tones is astonishing to us: months afterwards
they remembered the notes to which they had
been trained, responding correctly to one
of the other notes. Thus fishes have a good
absolute memory of tone, better indeed than
that of many human beings.
—Munro Fox, *The Personality*
of Animals

Until ten in the morning, the delicate mist continued
to hover over the horizon of Hanoi, a city of numerous lakes and verdant trees. I had finished my early
walk and reached the edge of Ho Chi Minh's lake,
tranquil and clear. I sat on the low rocky wall that
encircled it. In the place where I was sitting, it took

the form of a wide arc of smooth white limestone. A walkway made of the same rock cut through it, descending down to the water and sinking into it until it disappeared.

I prepared myself for a prolonged rest after my long walk, for which I had woken up at 5:00 a.m. I chose the spot closest to the walkway, where people thronged nonstop in order to see the miracle of the "Ho Chi Minh fish" that could be seen in this part of the lake. I was ready to experience them myself the moment the place was empty of visitors.

The vast light mist hovering above the ground cast a veil of enchantment over the spacious area around me, and through the luxuriant surrounding trees I could follow the most important (political) landmarks in Hanoi: the courthouse that had been the headquarters for the French governor before France's defeat in the Battle of Dien Bien Phu, the Museum of the Revolution, and the Mausoleum of Ho Chi Minh—the Ho Chi Minh whom I had finally seen, face to face, after a wait of more than thirty years.

At a distance of several steps from where I was sitting was the wooden home of Ho Chi Minh and behind it, the trench where the leadership of the Viet Cong used to meet to plan strategy for the Vietnamese resistance against the fiercest military fighting force in the world. Finally, a few meters away from where I was sitting was the unique wooden circular pergola with two tiers, which Ho Chi Minh had used exclusively for his time reading, for personal chats, and for the most important of the week's meetings, when a swarm of Hanoi children would come to spend a full day with him, a man who had never had children himself. He considered it the happiest day of his week.

As I sat by the edge of the lake and thought back on the events of the past five hours that morning in Hanoi, what leaped to mind was the moment I stood in front of Ho Chi Minh as he slept in peace, and in true beauty, within that sarcophagus of pure crystal flooded with light. Through persistent efforts, I had obtained permission to visit. I passed the first armed guard post, then the second, and then a third unarmed one. I conducted myself obediently, concealing all the nervousness I was feeling inside as I stood in the long queue of visitors on the broad extended avenue the size of a vast city square in front of the tomb. I advanced as though I were sleepwalking to climb the winding, dimly lit staircase. I crossed an anteroom where the light grew more intense with each step I took. Then I was brought to a halt with a light peremptory touch on my chest; with a similar touch on my back, I was invited to enter. I felt as though I were soaring close to the sky, in a preposterous, radiant dream.

Of all the international names that stood as lofty edifices in the time of my squandered left-wing youth, only the name of Ho Chi Minh remained with me. I spent four years in the Soviet Union, and whiled away dozens of hours in Red Square, but it never occurred to me, not even out of curiosity, to stand in the long queue that was swallowed up by the entrance to the dark polished stone tomb, within which rested the embalmed mortal remains of Lenin in a glass coffin. I visited Beijing and strolled for a long while in Tianan-men Square, mere steps from the hall where the body of Mao Zedong rested, embalmed in a glass coffin as well. I hesitated, but didn't take those few steps to look in on him. As for Ho Chi Minh, I had flown straight to him at the first glimmer of an opportu-nity, from the Near East to the Far East, across the entire expanse of Asia, in an exhausting journey, so I could wake up near dawn in Hanoi, armed with a trembling heart and a dewy eye, for a real, fleeting encounter with him.

He had decreed in his will that his comrades should bury him after he died, but they opposed his wishes in the name of "the right of the people to view the symbol of their freedom," and despite the boor-ishness of this "right," it afforded me one of the finest moments in my life. The poet whose ode to Ho Chi Minh's life I had loved in my youth didn't disappoint my imagination. Instead, Ho Chi Minh surpassed it, more than I could have ever thought. He was thin, of delicate frame, and with impressively formed fea-tures. The look on his face was peaceful. Hair com-pletely silver and silken. His eyes closed in serenity and repose. I remembered his finely worded formula on the problem of violence by the victim in opposi-tion to the tormentor's cruelty. I remembered what he

had said to the invading Americans: "I'm sorry . . .
you are coming to kill us, so we are forced to kill you.
It's a regrettable matter." Yes, a regrettable matter.

I recalled the asceticism of his life, his small por-
tions of food, his light clothing, and his sandals made
from the tires of American planes that his simple folk
had brought down. I thought that perhaps I was right
to keep my love for him all these years—a good memory from the distant days of my youth. I don't know
why I was thinking back on my political wander-
ings, on the edge of that lake named after him—they
were memories as far from politics as possible, but
all of them pleasant. Memories of people who had a
sweetness about them, with no obvious connection
between them other than that they were good human
beings. People whose natures were far removed from
violence and arrogance, but overflowing with compassion, tolerance, supportiveness, kind gestures,
sociability, friendship, confession, and forgiveness. I
had just cast myself back to the memory of my grandmother's kindnesses when I noticed the place around
me was empty. There was no one there on the stone
walkway leading down to the waters of the lake.

I got up to head toward the walkway and went
down it to the open area abutting the water. I stood
there, repeating what people had been doing in front
of me the whole time, in imitation of Ho Chi Minh,
when he would approach to feed the small purple fish
that he raised in the waters of the lake. Whenever he

clapped four times for them, they would swim to the surface, lifting their heads out of the water with their small mouths open, and take what he offered them.

I clapped four times. No fish appeared on the surface of the water near me. I clapped a second time and waited, but they didn't appear. I clapped and waited a third time, and a fourth time. Then I started clapping too quickly and with too much impatience. The only thing that stopped me was hearing a voice in an unassuming tone coming from behind me. It was speaking broken English on an Asian tongue: "They won't show like that."

I understood what the sentence meant: that the small purple fish in the lake wouldn't reveal themselves to me. I turned around to see one of the security guards looking down at me from the second-floor balcony in the wooden pergola.

I turned to him to ask, "Why won't they show themselves to me?"

"Because you are clapping without having food for them," he said. "I see you aren't carrying anything."

"Can the fish see me from underwater?" I asked him in annoyance.

"They know," he replied, with an irrefutable modesty. "They feel it."

I remembered that the fish had shown themselves to other people before me. They had clapped, the fish appeared, and they threw them food from small bags they pulled out of their pockets, or from under their arms. Some of them tossed leftover crumbs of bread from the food they'd eaten. There was always food at the end of the four claps.

I cast a sorrowful glance at the waters of the lake as I left. I was thinking about the fact that I would need to bring something with me. So I could feed the fish, if fate brought me back here again.

Mules

When the caliph al-Ma'mun was informed of
the disordered state of the empire's post-
al-relay network, he turned to Thumama ibn
Ashras, so he could look into that for him.
When he returned, al-Ma'mun questioned
him, and he replied, "Commander of the
Faithful, I was heading down a road, and
lo and behold, there was a mule who was
attacking a man who was wearing a green
head shawl. The mule thought it was a bun-
dle of fodder, so he went after the man, and
the man in turn started attacking the mule.
'Take off your head shawl!' I shouted to the
man. And when he took it off, the mule stood
there sniffing it."

—al-Jahiz, *On Mules*

I was amazed by a tribe who, when they were
asked, "Who is your father?" replied, "Our
mother is a horse."

—al-Jahiz, *The Book of Animals*

The mule is the offspring of a horse and a
donkey. If sired by a donkey, then it strongly
resembles a horse. If sired by a horse, then
it strongly resembles a donkey. It is amazing
that all of its parts are a cross between a

horse and a donkey, including its disposition.
It doesn't have the intelligence of the horse,
nor the dull-wittedness of the donkey. The
same goes for its braying and its gait. There
is no doubt about its sterility, but some say
of them, "The mule's fetus does not attach
to its mother's womb, and if a person eats
a mule's brain, then all his senses decline,
until he ends up in a sleeping state. A woman
who eats a mule's brain will never become
pregnant."
                    —al-Qazwini, *The Wonders*
                    of Creation

He woke up early, as usual, but he wasn't in a happy
mood when he stepped out of his private corporal's
tent. He opened wide his arms, his eyes, and his mouth
to the vastness of the awesome vista around him: the
mountains arrayed one after the other before his
eyes in captivating gradations of color, starting with
green, then olive, then purple, until, on the distant
horizon, they took on the color of blue-gray smoke;
the valleys following in succession down below, beneath the mountains' peaks; and the courses taken
by narrow paths that wound around the high eleva-
tions and that flowed out into the riverbeds. Farhan
didn't perform his morning exercises in celebration
of the fresh, clean air of these surroundings the way
he usually did—by himself, with enthusiasm, high

spirits, and noise. Nor did he go around afterward in an excellent mood, heading toward the soldiers' big tent, in order to cheerfully wake up the members of the border post, as he had done in the past: "Let's go, you donkeys—you and him! Wake up! . . . Look at these half-asleep mules!" Nor did anyone at the post banter with him as they came out of the tent, stretching and yawning, and say to him with a wink, "Yes sir, corporal, I can see. The mules are up . . . they've been up since dawn!" The private who made the joke didn't run off, and the corporal didn't run off after him. There was no undisciplined fraternizing of the kind that this mountain border outpost had often witnessed before.

Today, Corporal Farhan woke up in an unhappy mood. Anxiously and reluctantly, he assembled the members of the outpost for morning roll call. And with a heavy heart, he gave them the orders they were to carry out:

"A smuggling convoy is expected to pass by here at twelve noon . . . Your orders are to eliminate the contraband and the smugglers. Nothing—not a trace—will be confiscated or inspected. No questions asked, no explanations given."

He had received the signal on the radio the evening before. He had slept fitfully, and even those moments of sleep he had snatched for himself were riven by nightmares. He had seen himself running in terror, his back covered in flames. He had dreamed he had an enormous belly and he was propping up the mountain

with it, while his camouflage uniform was made of
steel. But there was someone cutting into the mountain from the opposite side with a giant drilling ma-
chine. He expected that person to reach his stomach
at any moment. Perhaps the drill holes and the flames
in his dream were inspired by the order he had been issued. It was an unusual order, one that had never been
given before. Even those few times he had received
orders to shoot, the shots were only of the buckshot
variety, in order to bring smugglers to a halt without
causing substantial injuries. Because at the end of the
day smugglers were living beings that ought to arouse
sympathy in the hardest of hearts—hearts that belonged to people with unpleasant voices, issuing orders to him and others like him from their glass-walled
offices in the distant capital. The smugglers were living
beings who were unaware of what they were transporting, and had no idea what it was meant for: they
were only dumb mules, stubborn and patient.

No other animal could traverse steep mountain
passes on their own like they could, without a human
leading them. Surefooted and hardy, they were excellent at crossing rugged mountain paths invisible to
the eye. Shrewd mule drivers trained them to make
their way through these wild places. They lived in
remote mountain villages scattered among the peaks
and lower slopes of this mountain range that marked
the border between the two countries. On one side, a
country opened up to everything, and on the other, a
country closed to the outside world. The mules were

trained to benefit a wide network of smugglers between the two countries, in spite of the difference
between the two regimes. On one side of the border the mules were loaded up with imported goods
and products that were embargoed on the other side.
The mules traveled without stopping for a full half-
day until they reached their destination. At first, the
journeys taken by smuggling mules were done under
cover of darkness. But once the smugglers' ring pen-
etrated the web of high officials in the government,
nighttime was no longer necessary for these wordless,
profitable trips. The smuggling mule convoys began
crossing mountain passes in broad daylight, just as
they had done at night—in fact, under the protection of the border posts themselves, which took their
share, either in the form of regular cash payments secretly sent to them from the smugglers, or via raids
on convoys when they hadn't been issued clear orders
to allow them to pass in peace, either because they
hadn't paid them off or they hadn't paid enough. The
contraband came in all shapes and sizes, and all of it
coincided with whatever was in short supply or was
hard to find in the country that was closed in on itself.
Most of it consisted of materials and equipment that
were illegal to import, but which could be found in
abundance in the homes of government officials and
influential people. Much of the contraband was similar to what that country itself produced, although the
crises that kept it in short supply were man-made. All
these things Farhan had learned by watching, when

he and his soldiers covertly observed what the convoy was carrying while they turned a blind eye as it passed nearby. Or he learned it through looting convoys, when they would pretend to confiscate goods, or from those convoys where they would make a point of looting a little. *What could this convoy possibly be carrying that they don't want us to let it through or even confiscate it? Drugs? Weapons? Snakes? Crap?* Farhan continued turning it over in his mind as he asked himself questions, took deep breaths, exhaled loudly, and spat on the ground, until a soldier on watch announced the first sighting of the convoy.

It was close to midday, and the mules appeared just as the message said they would, but they were still on the other side of the border, which meant Farhan and his men weren't permitted to deal with them right away. That was ideal for Farhan, as it allowed him to complete the order as it had been issued to him: he was not to let the soldiers change the ammunition in their weapons until the last moment. He gathered his soldiers together and had them empty out the regular bullets in their rifles, replacing them with different ammo. As soon as the first soldier took some of the new bullets to load into his weapon, he raised his voice nervously: "Incendiary bullets?!"

"Not a word out of you, soldier!" the corporal yelled at him. "Carry on! The orders say no questions, and no talking." Yes, it was true: they had said, *No questions.* They also said, *Open fire when the convoy is at the well.*

The convoy began to approach along the high mountain pass, about fifteen minutes' distance from the border post's campsite. That meant that the convoy would reach the well in twenty-five minutes, since the high pass wound around the nearest peak opposite the one the border post was on. The pass then descended gradually to the depth of the valleys before ascending again, heading toward another elevated pass, and wound around the next peak. The well was an unusually sunken spot in the valley nearest the border post. It really did resemble a well, since it dropped down suddenly to the bottom. The deep hollow was flat for a short distance, then climbed up sharply once again, to level off with the rest of the valley. It was a vast pit that was impossible for anything to get out of, except for mules, who could climb out of it in spite of the heavy loads on their backs: they stumbled and slipped sometimes, and climbed uphill with a bray of protest, but not for a moment did they stop moving forward until they emerged from it. This time there were strict orders that the mules would not be coming out. The well was located in a vertical drop directly below Corporal Farhan's post. So when they reached the well, the mules and their loads would be directly in range, and a very easy shot for his soldiers and their guns. They wouldn't need to aim carefully; they only had to point the muzzles down and keep pressing the trigger, to rain shots down on their targets without missing.

The next twenty minutes were the longest Farhan had spent in his rough, simple life. For ten years, he had been a commanding officer in the border garrison, the last four of them in this post above the well. So often he had counted himself fortunate to have been assigned this post! True, he had paid to be transferred to it, but soon enough he realized how lucrative it was. The post offered a substantial income, whether from the cash that came to him in unmarked envelopes that he surreptitiously got from the provisions corporal, whose truck passed by every month to supply the post with what they needed, or from smuggled goods, from which he was permitted to help himself a little, whenever confiscation orders were issued. He realized many people would describe someone like him as corrupt or bribable—even his soldiers whispered it among themselves, and he didn't object to them getting a piece of what he got. But he was the father of ten children, with a wife; an elderly, sick mother; and an invalid sister: he had thirteen mouths to feed in his distant village. He had acted as his own mufti and issued a religious ruling for himself: "There's nothing wrong with taking from thieves." And what was he getting, compared to what the big-shot smugglers got in their luxury offices, far from here? The big shots who ran the whole game? For a long time, he thought the whole thing was nothing more than a game, but now he felt the game was about to turn frighteningly serious once the convoy reached the well.

Twenty minutes passed as the convoy of mules drew closer. When they got as close as they were going to get, they would be two hundred meters away. Even so, Farhan still felt that these creatures, as they approached with their heavy loads, would turn their eyes directly to his—their big, round eyes that shared the kindly look in donkeys' eyes and the gleam in the kohl-black eyes of horses. When they blinked, he would be able to feel the touch of their long lashes directly on his bare heart. They reminded him of the eyes of his children in his faraway village along the riverbank, when they gathered around him during his time on leave. He got leave at widely spaced intervals: one week out of every four. Two days of the week's leave were taken up with getting there and returning, which left him only five days to spend with his children. They were never far from him during those five days. They never stopped looking directly at his eyes with their own, until they dropped off to sleep.

During those twenty minutes, despite the bright sunlight and his changed viewing position, he could only see the eyes of the animals in the convoy as they headed toward the well. He didn't see the chain of mountain peaks lit by the midday sun as it illuminated the mountains' colors in all their fascinating variety. It revealed the spectrum of colors on bare boulders chiseled by the winds, washed by the rains, and split by the hand of earthquakes from time immemorial. Magnificent layers of color, one after the other from bottom to top, and from top to bottom, in pink and gray shading into blue. There were green surfaces of verdant brilliance in those places where natural springs flowed, creating grassy areas perched in rocky crevices. He didn't see the outlines of the paths, the narrow defiles, the long trails painted by sunlight in white shading into red, as they twisted, climbed, and descended in a long beautiful ribbon running through this primordial mountain world. He didn't see the airy white clouds passing so close he could almost reach out and touch them. He didn't see the purest blue of the clearest sky high above the colorations of the lofty mountaintops. He saw only those wide, kohl-black eyes with long lashes looking into his. And after the fastest five minutes he had ever spent there, he found the convoy of mules, weighted down by the mysterious loads on their backs, coming downhill, as though they were sliding into the well that now held them all. Through the fog of his brain, he guessed there were more than ten of them.

He found the soldiers he had selected standing along the edge, holding their guns in a position of readiness. They were looking at him with an inquisitive silence. He saw their eyes coming closer, staring at his eyes as they held their positions. The eyes of the dumb animals in the well were directed at him and coming closer, too. He felt nauseous. He was terrified of falling into that well of eyes. "Weapons!" he burst out, as though shouting a cry for help from the dark depths of his broad, hairy chest. All that was left was to give the order to fire.

The Sadness of Horses

I have seen in *The History of Nishapur* by
Judge Abu Abdallah, in the biography of
Abu Ja'far al-Hasan ibn Muhammad ibn
Ja'far al-Zahid al-Abid, a hadith that he
recounted which originated, via its chain of
transmitters, with Ali ibn Abi Talib (may
God be pleased with him.) According to
Ali, the Prophet said, "When God Almighty
wanted to create the horse, he told the south
wind, 'I am making a creature out of you,
which I will make into a source of glory
for My followers, a humiliation for My
enemies, and an object of beauty for those
who obey Me.' The wind replied, 'Create, O
Lord.' So He seized a handful of the wind,
and from it created a horse. Then God said,
'I have created you a true Arabian. I have
caused excellence to be woven into your
forelocks and spoils of war to be won on
your back, and I have provided you with
ample sustenance. I have made you superior
to other beasts of burden, and have filled
your master with affection for you. I have
caused you to fly without wings, for you are
good at pursuing and fleeing. I shall place
upon your back men who will glorify Me,

praise Me, say the *shahada* in My name,
and say the *takbir* for Me.'"
—al-Damiri, *Major Compendium
on the Lives of Animals*

Changes in their environment often frighten
horses. Skittish horses even appear to be
alarmed by imagined changes: an object
that a horse has passed countless times may
suddenly cause a horse to shy although there
has been no alteration.
—Jeffrey Moussaieff Masson
and Susan McCarthy, *When
Elephants Weep*

The horse I was riding in the middle of the minefield
didn't stumble, so I couldn't say he slipped. He didn't
instantly throw me off his back, and he didn't fling
me to the ground without warning. Instead, I discovered, while we were in the middle of the road, that
he was slowing down. He was intent on slowing his
pace, then he came to a standstill, as though he had
been turned off. He remained motionless like that for
a few moments, and then began to drop to the ground
beneath me. He tipped over as he fell, falling flat on
his side. I found myself beside him on the sand, flat on
my back, my hand squeezing tight to the handle of my
doctor's bag, which hadn't fallen open. My body was
immobile in the position I had fallen in. I was frozen

in place like a statue and, dazzled by the glare of day-light, I could hardly see. My pupils must have dilated as wide as possible in those moments, because the pale sand suddenly went shiny. The sky looked pure white, and the surface of the ocean that surrounded the island on all sides sparkled, like a mirror polished to rival the light of the sun—the same sun that blazed in the skies above, in my eyes, and on my skin, which I could feel was getting burned.

I was struck by a sensation of inner heat, and sweat poured out of me. My brain felt like it was melting. No mine had exploded—of that I was certain. I realized that the sparks flooding over me were only reflections of the fear and surprise inside me. I was disoriented, swarmed by a million images—of dying by explosion, mosquito stings, or thirst; of living as an amputee; and of being rescued, all at the same time. Then, little by little, I began to grow cold. My mind grew clear as, in the total silence, I heard a muffled sound. I couldn't believe I was hearing it. Slowly, cautiously, I stretched out my hand toward the horse's muzzle. I could feel his warm, moist breaths, one after another. I stood up with a leap and cried out, "He's not dead! He's not dead! He's not dead!"

My spirit jumped with joy at being saved, but soon enough it sank in despair at what came next, because as soon as I bent down next to the horse's head to look him over and run my hands over him, I realized that even if he wasn't dead, he was on the point of death. He was lying motionless where he had fallen, and would stay like that until he died. The spark had gone out of his half-closed eyes and his eyelids weren't blinking. His breaths came feebly through his nostrils, which slackened in exhaustion.

Before I'd ever set foot on this island, I had heard about this phenomenon from my veterinarian colleagues but didn't believe it. Hesitantly, I touched the cornea of the horse's eye with my fingertip. He didn't blink. The hair on his mane grew stiff, but he didn't move. Out of my bag I took out a needle to test his senses. I began sticking it deeply into the horse's body in a number of places. He didn't show the slightest reaction. He had listlessly dropped to the ground and would stay like this until he died. And I in my turn would die, too: even if I tried to walk by myself, I would risk setting off one of the many mines the Israelis had laid on the island when they briefly overran it. Even if I stayed just where I was, death would come to me by sunstroke, or snakebite, or from the tail of a scorpion, the kind that never stops scurrying, black against the surface of the sands. Even if they noticed my absence and started looking for me, by the time they found me I would be a corpse, or as good as one.

My despair knew no bounds: the only thing I could do was submit to the likelihood of death. I threw myself down on my back next to the motionless horse and stared at the sky, which was regaining its blue color. And as I stared, I mulled over images . . .

⁂

My God, how invigorated I was by the call for assistance that reached our hospital from the island. They were sending for a doctor to supervise an "unexpected condition" in a patient. It was as though I had been waiting for this summons. I begged to be the one to respond. My colleagues were taken aback by my insistence, since most of them didn't like assignments involving the sea, or those desolate, isolated islands far from shore. They were even more surprised when they learned that I requested to stay overnight on the island, since the patient's condition didn't require me to accompany him on an immediate transfer to the hospital.

How often I had felt myself drawn to this island, without having ever set foot on it. It appeared like a phantom on the water's horizon when the sky was cloudless, and when the waves were high and fog rose up over the water, it disappeared as though it had never existed. The island was surrounded by a halo of stories, amid the sea teeming with colorful fish, voracious sharks, gardens of alluringly colored coral reefs. The island's celebrated lighthouse was where the "Captain," who had only a small number of soldiers with him, held out against the Israelis when they invaded the island. He and his men all died fighting the hostile landing that had been preceded by an aerial bombardment and that was armed to the teeth with armored amphibious vehicles and heavy artillery. The landing parties made it up to the lighthouse but it continued to hold out, which led them to estimate it held an entire company. Ammunition in the light-house ran out, and they bombarded its position with intense firing that was strong enough to melt an ar-mored car, before they advanced on it. They were sur-prised to find a single man who had only one weapon and was bleeding profusely. They didn't give him the salute a brave warrior deserves, as is the custom of all armies and military traditions; instead, they unloaded more bullets into his bleeding body, and gouged out his eyes as he lay dying. Then they tossed him from the top of the lighthouse so his body would be torn to pieces on the pitiless sea-sprayed boulders below. The island now bore his name, although its former name—simply "the Island"—was still widely used. It was an island surrounded by turquoise-blue waters, revealing a delicate, enchanting necklace of colorful sea corals encircling it, like a frame of light amid the dark blue of the deep waters. An island where they say gazelles can be seen—gazelles brought there by the former king when he used to visit the island. He left them behind and forgot about them, and then time forgot about him. Changing eras and people's short memories left the gazelles behind. It's said that they reveal themselves from time to time, like gentle, fleet-footed dreams. They appear for a few moments, then scatter, on an island that the Israelis, out of spite, had transformed into a minefield shortly before they were driven off it. Walking about freely is still deadly there, except on horses with trained senses and a delicate gait, horses selected from the best Arabian

breeds, who know their way through safe riverbeds;
horses that are good at dancing to melodies played
on a *mizmar*, to the song of a reed pipe or the rhythm
of a tambourine. Their bodies are a marvel of sym-
metry, their eyes are beautiful and coal black, and
their gait rises and falls to a beat, corresponding to
music that can be as intricate as a half-beat and quarter tone. The horses are like beautiful maidens whose
beauty only increases when they are cared for and
pampered, and whose unattractiveness grows with
rough and cruel treatment. The horses are adept at
cutting narrow paths between the mines, just as they
are skilled at prancing between notes and quarter
notes. But they couldn't endure what life on the island entailed; they couldn't endure the dry sands, the
arid rocks, the tedium of the sea's continuous roar,
the glimmering of the water, or the roughness of its
inhabitants, whose life on the island had taught them
to become accustomed to silence, to take refuge in
long periods of sleep, or to roam in endless, empty
waking dreams. The horses became depressed on the
island, and their depression was as violent as they
were delicate. They surprised their stable hands,
young men who had little experience with horses,
by leaping into the ocean and swimming frantically,
until they reached the places where sharks gathered.
Shutting their eyes to those murderous, lidless eyes,
they submitted their long, delicate, arched necks
and their elegant hindquarters to the ravenous jaws,
which become crueler and sharper when the ocean

water is dyed red with blood. Several horses killed themselves this way, vanishing completely into the voracious bellies of sharks in a matter of minutes. Those horses that were prevented from jumping into an abattoir of sharks would commit suicide on land in a less dramatic fashion, and with a stubborn intransigence: they would collapse suddenly and lie motionless on the ground until they died, dehydrated, of thirst and hunger.

I was recalling stories about the island as I stood on the deck of the launch that took me there. We crossed the expanse of shallow turquoise waters along the coastal strip and began to make our way into the blue depths. We encountered swarms of red mullet, which appeared like sparks of silver and copper, a glitter that flew in a wide arc above the water then plunged to conceal itself beneath the waves. In the deep blue waters crowned with white wave crests, the smooth, energetic bodies of dolphins flashed by, making cheerful leaps. And in the deepest blue, almost black, waters, there were waves that concealed within their farthest depths sea beasts whose jaws were filled with rows of triangular teeth, tapered like sawblades. Not a single one came into view, not even the tip of a dorsal fin through the water, but the smooth dark whirlpools in this area revealed their deadly presence.

As we navigated farther into the deep waters, we saw the blue become lighter, as seagulls circled overhead, white in the brilliance of the sun. Then the island suddenly appeared as though it had just risen from the bottom of the sea. As soon as our boat touched the wooden dock extending from the island's quay, I found three men waiting for me, accompanied by a Beni Jameel horse. A sense of excitement welled up in me, and I took a great leap onto the dock before the launch came to a complete stop and was secured.

The men on the dock welcomed me. The effects of isolation and a prolonged lack of access to fresh food were apparent on them: skinny bodies, dark skin gone sallow, and light-colored blotches on their face. They talked slowly, their voices coming out cracked and low. I asked them about the sick man, and they answered that the horse would take me to him on the other end of the island. I noticed that the horse hadn't been tied up, and that no one was holding on to it. Instead, it just stood there quietly, although it was restless for some reason. One of the men saw me looking uncertainly at the horse. "He knows the way by heart," he said, reassuring me. "Knows it by heart."

I saw a wooden kiosk there—it was clearly for the dock guard—with an ancient telephone. I asked them if the telephone was working, and if I could call the patient or his relatives. The telephone worked with an efficiency belied by its dilapidated appearance and rusty surface. I inquired about the symptoms the patient was exhibiting, and determined that his condition didn't require surgery, nor did it call for his immediate transfer to our hospital in the city. I prescribed for him a double injection of pain reliever and antispasmodic to be administered when I got to him. I felt pleased that I had plenty of time ahead of me, so I could take my time getting a feel for life on the island and for its stories.

I mounted the horse, and one of the men handed me my doctor's bag as I sat astride its back. If I hadn't unleashed a barrage of questions on the three men before setting out, they wouldn't have told me anything I needed to have explained to me, either because they were taciturn and indifferent, or because they were certain that nothing would happen that would expose me to danger. In response to my questions, they told me I should never spur on the horse to speed it up, especially in the heavily mined area, which I would reach in fifteen minutes, and that I shouldn't hit or touch his neck, on either side, lest he deviate from his course, and I shouldn't sing on the road or hum, so as not to stir him up and make him trot from side to side or prance—he might step on a mine that would blow us both up! I got the impression from them that I should be asleep, or half-asleep, on the horse's back, and leave it to his vigilance alone to get me there safe and sound. It seems that this idea became a kind of autosuggestion, and I was on the verge of actually lulling myself to sleep when I noticed that the horse was moving slowly, just as I was drifting into drowsiness. When I lifted my head to force myself awake, I found that the horse had come to a halt. My alarm doubled when he proceeded to fall over and toss me down next to him.

The heat of midday passed over our heads, with the scorching sand beneath us. I began to feel thirst burning my throat, although the watch on my wrist indicated that not more than fifty minutes had passed since I left the harbor—that is, that thirty-five minutes had passed since the horse toppled over. He was still lying on his side motionless, unblinking and unresponsive to stimuli, even after I repeatedly poked him with a needle in his veins until he bled. Despair began to assail me and penetrate my being, finally reaching the point of sardonic humor—a bitter humor, for I knew it to be true of myself, as with most of my family, that when we've reached the limit of despair, we have a tendency toward self-derision. We make jokes. I began to joke with the horse, rubbing its neck and the wavy, abundant hair on its mane, speaking to it in a gentle tone: "Hey there, you stupid horse . . . You only get one life, and you want to die. Don't you know that beyond this island there's an ocean, and beyond the ocean there's a shore? And on the shore are green pastures, rippling with delicious grass? Streams with water as sweet as sugar run through them. And there are incredibly beautiful horses there, with dewy-eyed glances . . . oh, you stupid horse!" I continued to rub its neck with my palm, talking about those green pastures. I got lost in thought as I made a place for people there, too—or, to be precise, for myself, where I would meet most of those who I loved, and get the best of what I desired. I became so engrossed in my singsong reverie, it became a dream. The dream took on solid form and turned into real feelings. I was on the verge of bringing it to life and living in it myself, seeing as I was hemmed in by a narrow circle with death on every side. All of a sudden, I felt the touch of the horse's neck change, felt its hair grow ticklish in the palm of my hand, and felt its muscles throb, like nerves set in motion when tensed. I leaned over him to look at his head, and found that he had opened his eyes, which gleamed with a marvelous radiance. I continued to sing to him and massage his neck, as though I were singing to myself and massaging my spirit. In fact, I *had* been singing to myself and massaging my spirit—and lo and behold, the horse got up from its lifeless sprawl on the ground. He righted himself, straightening his legs and lifting his head, as though waking from a deep slumber. He stood up, with me hanging on to his neck. I couldn't believe what had happened. How did it happen? Why did it happen? Was it the act of massaging the nerve endings in his body that made his sensory apparatus, which had shut itself down in preparation for death, come to life again, in order to prepare itself to continue living? When I was doing my medical internship on rotation in pediatrics I had observed infants on the verge of death due to dehydration because their veins could no longer take liquid solutions intravenously. Then I would see them drink those same solutions orally when they were held by their mothers, who rubbed their backs and poured out from the depths of their own souls a substance that improved their chances.

When I sang of that dream, did my voice turn into a summons whose words were meaningless because its meanings were wrapped up in the intonations of my voice? Did my singsong voice reverberate and affect my own inner self, so that I felt myself drawn to this reverberation, as though it had become an end in itself, complete in and of itself?

I noticed the horse's breaths, quite close to my head, as I stood beside him. I saw him lift his ears and perk up his mane and the hair of his long, beautiful tail, as though he were inviting me to get up on him. I mounted him, although I had forgotten the men's warnings at the harbor, that I shouldn't touch the sides of the horse's neck. I was patting the side of his neck and rubbing my palm on it when he began to prance as though he were moving in time to an Eastern melody played on silent woodwinds, reeds, and tambourines. In my heart, I didn't have the slightest fear that his step might go wrong: I had forgotten all the talk about mines, as if I'd never heard it. I was enveloped in a strange feeling of intoxication, as though I weren't riding a horse that was walking on the ground, but a magic carpet that took me soaring above the clouds. I hoped the flight would never end, but the patient was waiting for me at the other end of the island.

The sun's disc rose big and red from the bosom of the waters, fighting back the early morning twilight of violet mist. I was up with the seagulls as I made contact again with the city. Having carried out my mission and reassured myself about the patient, I asked for the launch to be sent to bring me back. I had seen everything I wanted to see on the island, and my curiosity was gone. I had seen what people see, what people don't see, and what they could see if they wished to. I saw the island's surface covered in magically smooth white sand, from the finely ground powder of coral reefs strewn about by millions of colored parrot-fish beaks. Powder now dry and gleaming white with the passage of eons, although reference works claim that its surface is rocky and devoid of life. I saw the lighthouse illuminated, although everyone was certain that it had been dark for many long years. I saw the gazelles, which they think are a mirage, but they were no mirage.

In the morning, they told me the launch had arrived to bring me back, so I rode the horse—the same horse—to the other end of the island, where the harbor was. I repeated the journey I had made the day before with greater care, repeated the pats and massages on the side of the neck that they had warned me not to touch, the incantation we had shared between ourselves in a dream, and the intonations that have no need of words. With a prancing gait, the horse jauntily took me through the minefields. I wasn't afraid of his prancing or his high spirits. I found the launch ready to depart from the harbor, so I got down from the horse. He neighed as though he were saying something, or wanted to speak. And when the launch sped off on its return trip, leaving behind the thin surface of turquoise water, heading toward the deep blue, I heard the horse neighing behind me. I turned around. He was rearing up, raising his legs high in the air, as if he were calling to me. The men surrounded him, as they struggled to control him and bring him down.

Water Buffalo

The water buffalo is a mighty animal that
does not sleep at all, although perhaps at some
times during the night he closes his eyelids.
They say that there is a worm in his brain that
is always moving and never lets him sleep. He
can defend himself from a lion, and can kill
a crocodile with the great mass of his body,
which is why water buffalo graze freely along
the edge of the Nile. The water buffalo will
walk right up to the lion, for he has an un-
flinching heart. To defend himself, he has only
his horns, which have no sharp edges compared to the sharpness of the lion's claws and
fangs, but still he defeats the lion. They say,
*The water buffalo defeats the lion because he
can chase the lion away, even though the lion
wants to make a meal out of him.*
—al-Qazwini, *The Wonders
of Creation*

Casualties

Nine people, ten water buffalo, fifteen lambs and
goats, and a large indeterminate number of chickens.

Rabbits were not among the casualties, for reasons that no one bothered to explain. Among inanimate objects, seven houses had fire damage, two of which were entirely consumed by the flames. Three grocery storefronts were destroyed, the facades of eight dried-mud houses were demolished, and all the barn fencing collapsed. After midnight, the manure piles and haystacks were scattered like dust in the sky over the village, and they didn't settle down until dawn, when they slowly and gradually descended, to blanket houses and people overcome by exhaustion and terrified by the catastrophic events. They wept dry tears, without wailing over the victims, whom they started preparing for burial that morning: two men (one aged thirty and the other approaching eighty), two middle-aged women (one of them nine months pregnant), and five children, whose ages ranged between six months and eleven years.

Lights

The neon lights began their relentless takeover of the village's night sky twenty years ago, ever since the broadcasting signal-boosting station began emitting its radio waves out of the small newly constructed building surrounded by walls along the main road in front of the village. The workers who had taken jobs at the station were local villagers. They had been impoverished farm laborers who neither owned nor rented the land they tilled. Those who owned or rented land hired them to work for them during the harvest season. These station employees passed on word to the rest of the village about what they had discovered after they had worked out the secret of the station from the engineers and technicians there. They understood that the station's antennas were sending out strong waves that carried on their backs the transmission waves that had grown weak after coming all the way from the radio building in the distant capital. They called those signal-boosting waves "donkeys" because of their strength, their steadfastness, and their endurance as they supported the exhausted broadcasting waves and carried them all the way to the coast. As these "donkey" waves launched into the air currents that crossed the village sky, they gave off enough electricity into the atmosphere to light burned-out neon lamps, which had nothing left in them except a little mercury gas—not enough for the electricity in the wires, the current converters, or the usual starter coils to make the bulb glow.

The Relentless Advance of Lights

Over the course of twenty years, the neon lights accumulated. It cost nothing for the villagers to light their broken lamps. They didn't need electrical connections or any rigging other than just hanging them up on walls, near rooftops, over fences, and between tree branches. They didn't need cords to string them up, just whatever was handy—fiber ropes, shreds of tattered clothing, or even linen threads and ivy vines.

An Excess of Incandescence

Within a year, give or take a little, the village lights had begun to glow brighter at night, until the village became one of the most—if not *the* most—brightly lit spots on earth. Its nights had become days illuminated by several suns. The widespread use of energy-saving daylight lamps in the country's cities began to put neon lights—even when they were still at full capacity—into early retirement. Working neon lights grew numerous in the village, at almost no cost. They didn't need to be hung up for the electricity in the air of the village to connect to their cathodes and light up their abundant gas. Their mere presence, hung up anywhere with both sides exposed, guaranteed they would glow brightly, on the ground, in the streets and alleys, over the fences and rooftops, in the animal pens, inside the chicken coops, over the canal bridges, and in all the fields.

The Change Wasn't Unexpected

Things went on like that for two decades, even if its growth was gradual and its features expanded over time. The village's harvests, flooded by sunlight during the day and by neon lights at night, grew faster, larger, taller, and more abundant, although produce lost its familiar flavor. Cows began eating night and day without stopping, ending up closer to elephants in size, and they provided copious amounts of thin milk. However, their offspring became extremely weak: most of their calves perished in the first few days after birth. As for the people, their bodies grew obese, and they were inclined to be flabby and sluggish when they moved. Their sleep patterns became a series of short naps over the course of the day. During the brightly lit nights they no longer retired to their bedrooms in the evening to sink into sleep until early morning, the way they used to. Instead, they began to stretch out on stone benches, on rooftops, and beneath trees, to sleep in snatches at different times, only to wake up hungry and yawning, so they could eat and work a little. Then they would go back and stretch out again when their eyelids grew heavy.

The Night of the Storm

It was said that the strength of the current in the station's converters had a sudden spike. It was also said that that's not what happened, but rumor had it that the neon lights that blanketed the village and the surrounding fields grew unusually bright, such that owls suddenly nodded off on sycamore branches and fences and fell crashing down hard to earth. Bats returned to the roofs and eaves of ruined buildings, and clung there like suction-cup darts stuck to their targets. Bees began to buzz more, and birds, whose flying was disturbed, began to chirp louder. An unfamiliar clamor arose in the henhouses and pigeon coops, and the corrals grew noisy.

At Thirty Minutes Past Midnight

Enormous frustrated poundings caused the doors of the corrals to fly off and tore apart their mud walls. The village's water buffalo—all of them—burst free through the collapsed doors and the holes in the walls, as though a demon had summoned them all in a single moment. They were transformed into a stampeding herd, rushing blindly and madly into Farm Access Road, which ran through the entire length of the village. When the herd, rushing headlong, reached the end of the long road, it found itself in front of the old wooden bridge over the drainage canal, which was quickly destroyed under the weight of the animals and the heavy stomping of their hooves.

Following the Collapse of the Bridge

Several water buffalo fell into the waters of the canal, and the agitated herd shuddered to a halt, as the shock of the unexpected standstill began to make its way through the crowded body of buffalo, which were now colliding with each other. The shock combed through the herd from beginning to end, as muzzles and horns began to turn around, get tangled up and butt against each other. The great herd broke up into small, chaotic groups that ran off in every direction. Wherever a light flashed here or there, the frenzied water buffalo turned their heads in that direction, toward any place where neon lights were hung or could be found. And when it was difficult for them to get to a lamp in an enclosed space, they proceeded to ram themselves against walls or doors or fences. In fact, they began poking their way into alleys and bursting into homes, searching for that glowing white light in order to extinguish it with their horns, their hooves, their snouts, and their rumps. They struck at emanations of that white light with all the fury their massive bodies possessed. The lights began to dim while fires burned, dust flew up, people screamed, and chickens and livestock tried to flee. But the trampling continued. When it became clear that they were aiming for those white lights, people hurried to smash all the lights their hands and legs could reach, until the village had gone completely dark, and the herds began making their way toward the only white lights that remained, the ones flickering in the wide expanse of the fields.

Enchanted Rabbits

We are—not metaphorically, but precisely,
biologically—like the doe nibbling moist
grass in the predawn misty light; chewing,
nuzzling a dewy fawn, breathing the foggy
air, feeling so much at peace; and suddenly,
for no reason, looking about wildly.
> —Melvin Konner, *The Tangled
> Wing*, quoted in Jeffrey Moussaieff
> Masson and Susan McCarthy,
> *When Elephants Weep*

Rabbits sleep with their eyes open. If a
hunter comes to them and finds them like
that, he will think they are awake. It is said
that if they see the sea, they die.
> —al-Damiri, *Major Compendium
> on the Lives of Animals*

I couldn't wait when I heard what they were saying
about the nocturnal apparition of those rabbits in our
city's old square, now that the main electrical generator had burned down and a pitch-black darkness
had descended over the square and its surroundings.

It looked as though it would stay that way for several days, until the generator could be repaired. I rode the last express train heading into the city so I could get there by twilight. The rabbits were said to make their strange appearance after midnight and to vanish completely with the first glimmers of dawn. Dozens, hundreds—some went so far as to claim thousands—of bright, dazzlingly white, rabbits would pour out under cover of darkness onto the wide old city square, when it was empty of people. They emerged from somewhere unknown and spread out without making a sound. They moved effortlessly with delicately trembling heads, their long ears slowly swaying, their mouths continuously nibbling on invisible grass, as if the dusty asphalt of the square had been turned into a giant pasture with plenty to eat.

Twenty-six years ago, fate and the innocence of youth made me the prime suspect in the events that befell the city on New Year's Day. The public prosecutor charged me with instigating the events, along with the subsequent destruction and threat to state security, including the shooting deaths of two citizens by persons unknown. The punishment which the prosecutor's office sought for me was life imprisonment at hard labor. The case dragged on for seven full months, which I spent in the city's prison, along with three students, the only ones not released out of the 150 who had been arrested during the events. I wasn't being "honored" with these serious charges because of any prominent role I had played, but rather because of political opportunism on the part of the authorities against a young man who treated politics with an artist's spirit: he professed what he believed was most honest and beautiful and called things what they were, dangerous as that was to do. He wasn't afraid to point fingers at great and weighty personages, never backing down from the reckless behavior that twenty of the best political lawyers, working pro bono, rallied to defend, in order to get him a not guilty ruling. His lawyers' sincere efforts proved their worth, and fate settled on an incorruptible judge: this case turned out to be the last one he would oversee before he went into retirement. He ruled that I was completely innocent of all charges, although this verdict could have been obtained with much less effort if I had been able to direct the attention of the judge and the lawyers to an incident that would have proven that the charges the prosecutor's office was making against me, fomenting destruction and chaos, were untrue. It was an incident that could have been confirmed by a few eyewitnesses—namely, an old gardener who was employed in the governor's mansion, and two students who were friends of mine.

Several weeks before the New Year's events broke out, I was pursuing one of the "romantic" pastimes of that era, in the rain. In the beautiful neighborhoods in the quiet part of the city—at least, it was quiet then—I was walking aimlessly along empty streets washed clean by the rain, gazing with dreamy eyes at balconies and windows. Having just lost the one I loved, I was musing about finding someone new to fall in love with. Near sunset, after the city's light rain had finished working its magic, turning the blue of the sky and the white of the marvelous houses below it into a dreamlike mirage, I walked past the governor's mansion, which was surrounded by high walls with concrete foundations, topped with sharp-pointed iron bars and obscured by reinforced panels of frosted glass. I was surprised to see a bright white rabbit running free through the door, which was slightly ajar. Chasing after the rabbit was a young woman: in my entire life I had never seen a girl as charming as she was. Right behind her, a group of military guards emerged in pursuit of the rabbit. I was walking directly in the path of this chase and found myself caught up in it. I no longer saw anything but the girl and the rabbit. The soldiers disappeared, as if they weren't there at all. Instinctively, I tried to grab the rabbit, which I started chasing with the energy of every cell in my body, now come to life. And indeed, I did catch it. I trapped it between the wall of the mansion and the pavement and threw myself at it with all I had. Its submissiveness and calmness took me by surprise. I was careful not to let it slip away as I lifted it up from where it sat crouched on the pavement by the fence. It seemed to share my sense of caution: rather than trying to wriggle out of my hands, it began to draw itself together to allow me to get a better grasp on it.

It lay completely still between my chest and forearms, where I gently cradled it. With the rabbit in my arms, I headed toward the girl, who approached me with a grateful smile. The glimpse of her smile and the softness of the delicate, warm, white fur in my arms was one of the most magical moments of my youth. From the corner of my eye, I could see the soldiers hurrying over, their hands outstretched to take the rabbit from me. But she waved them off and asked me to keep holding it so I could take it back where it belonged. They obeyed her decisive, calmly given orders.

Thus, for the first time in my life, I entered the governor's mansion, with a warm, bright white rabbit in my arms. My heart beat rapidly with joy and apprehension. I felt as though I were in a dream. The beautiful woman led me inside as the soldiers stared at me, stifling their anger. Their narrow eyes shot baleful glances, filled with veiled threats, in my direction. I had overstepped some line they couldn't put their finger on. The girl led me to a corner of the mansion's back garden, which looked out over the river. There I saw multi-tiered wire cages, in which sat dozens of bright white rabbits, just like the rabbit I was carrying. The beautiful woman opened a small wire door in a row of cages level with my chest and motioned to me to approach. I gently poured the rabbit through the gap she held open with her fingertips. I was close to her sweet face and felt intoxicated by her pure skin, which I grazed lightly, as though from far, far away. My legs nearly gave way beneath me, and would have, if not for the alarming presence of the soldiers. With pristine nails, she locked the door of the wire cage on the rabbit, now no longer up against my chest. She thanked me with a charming smile that I felt offered me a promise of something more. But a passage opened up in front of me through the group of soldiers, forming a path for me to leave, and I found myself outside the gate of the mansion, which slammed shut behind me. I headed off, staggering like someone who'd woken up while still in the middle of a dream, feeling light as air, as though the breezes were on the verge of carrying me aloft. I was determined to return to see the dream through to its close. And I did return—I returned time and time again. Undaunted, I circled around the mansion's walls, bristling with iron and made impenetrable by frosted glass, but to no avail, until the day I was able to enter the mansion again, but found only those rabbits inside!

Demonstrations broke out in our city the day after protests blazed up in the capital. On Tuesday evening, news from the capital reached the city, and the next morning, political graffiti, which I had helped to write the night before, covered the city's walls, demanding freedom and justice. Before noon, student demonstrations set out from the university, joined by the residents of lower-class neighborhoods. Floods of protestors broke through police barricades and provocations on Corniche Street and headed toward the provincial government building. Their numbers multiplied to tens and hundreds of thousands, and by midday, a rumbling octopus of half a million demonstrators filled the streets leading to the provincial government building from all directions. For some reason that lay within the spontaneous movement of the crowd, which was now beyond the students' control, the collective pressure zeroed in on the governor's mansion. I was there, excited, heart pounding, my spirit with the popular uprising in the street and my heart behind the concrete wall and the iron and frosted glass. The anger and suffering of the common people had been let loose. In a few seconds, the glass of the lights on the mansion's walls shattered and fell to the ground, and a few moments later all the frosted glass that obscured the view within went flying. The mansion was revealed, exposed to the street. There was no longer any trace of the soldiers I had encountered before. Lace curtains swung back and forth behind the glass windows, revealing feverish movement within. Some men appeared in civilian garb, hurrying in the direction of the garden overlooking the river. I was roused to action by a horrible notion that struck my brain, which I confided to some of my friends, the student leaders, who were standing near me: "This entire uprising will be stained with disgrace if there is any assault against a woman in the palace. The arrests will be bloody—and justifiable, even to people who have been sympathetic to the uprising so far." The noise was deafening, and it was difficult for us to hear each other. Through the congestion of sweaty faces, elated at discovering the pleasure of protest, I only succeeded in reaching the ears of two friends. The three of us tore through the crowds of demonstrators pressing up against the front of the gate, and we called out to some of the palace employees who we could see behind the bars of the fence as they hurried by. From their gesticulations, we understood that the palace's occupants had already left. From the swarm of people around us, we heard voices confirming that the governor had fled and that his family had been evacuated in a small boat to an unknown location across the river.

I became separated from my two friends in the crush, which was like an enormous millstone: it felt like it wasn't moving, but in fact it was rolling slowly, sweeping away everything in its path. I found myself directly in front of the entrance to the palace, with a gigantic human siege engine behind me, its frame composed of hundreds of thousands of people. They slowly backed up, shouting with one breath, Heave!, then advanced in one overwhelming mass, yelling Ho! as they slammed against the entrance, its door panels shackled with a thick steel chain and locked with a giant brass padlock. On one side of the chain running through the padlock, I noticed that one link had already come loose and was splitting open further with each blow of the surging human battering ram. The blows struck the armor-plated panels, and my ribs were slammed against its iron doorway. The palace appeared to be completely empty behind the iron bars of the entrance gate, which was on the verge of bursting open. But I was preoccupied with other thoughts: a vision flashed before my eyes of the white rabbits and the glistening river that bordered the palace garden . . . True, the governor was no longer there, and his family had been transported by motor launch to a safe place. But who could tell whether the girl of my dreams was a member of that family or not? Perhaps, in spite of her refined appearance and elegant clothes, she was merely an employee who worked in the palace, one of those young women who help at official ceremonies, carefully selected to make a good impression on palace guests. The palace was one of the nation's official guest residences, where presidents and kings stayed when they visited the city. Was she still there? Was she hiding in terror in a remote corner of the palace? Was it possible to reach her in some rash, wild way? I was filled with the spirit of heroism and self-sacrifice—two means to the same end. I decided to hinder the imminent collapse of the palace's main entrance until I could be more certain that the woman of my dreams had left the palace. I wound the chain back on itself when the fearsome battering ram receded to its lowest ebb, just before it returned with a terrifying surge and a stunning hammer blow. The surge caught me by surprise just as I was finishing my work, and the chain tore off a bit of flesh from my right index finger. I still have the scar today. The entrance gate creaked and groaned, and the chain quickly spun around itself. The two rings at the ends of the chain snapped, and the heavy padlock flew up into the air like a feather. Then the gate burst open, flinging wide its panels before the roaring flood of attackers. I was in the vanguard, struggling against the torrent, and I turned around shouting, "No assaults on women! No assaults on women!" But the flood overwhelmed me and my cries, and I found a friendly hand pulling me away from the rapid currents. It was an old man, one of the palace gardeners. "There's no one left, son," he told me. "No women, and no men." I gave his kindly old face a fleeting glance, and realized that he hadn't fled like the rest, confident that with his appearance and his age, not even the devil himself would be tempted to attack him. I ran like a madman, crashing against the crowd of attackers. I climbed a staircase, passing by rooms and running through opulent reception halls, empty except for the feverish anger of the dispossessed, who spread out everywhere like locusts. I headed downstairs, still running, and found myself in the garden overlooking the river. And there were the stacked wire rabbit cages, with hundreds of hands reaching out for them. The cages had been destroyed and dozens of rabbits had escaped. And to think that I had once carried one of them in my arms, in that waking dream!

※

I came back out through the entrance gate to follow what was happening on the street, struck by a sense of shame at staying inside. After the glass on the walls had been smashed and the palace's window panels had flown off, the protestors had completely pulled the pavement up from the street. Through the windows, I saw a series of frenzied scenes unfold one after the other: someone jumped up and swung from one of the giant chandeliers, then he fell and we heard a tinkling from the sound of crystal shattering on marble. More crashing sounds followed, although we couldn't see what was going on inside. One person yanked at the lace curtains to rip them down. He set fire to their edges, then dangled them, burning, from the windows. Pieces of expensive furniture were tossed out into the street, smashing to pieces below. Someone grabbed a gas pipe, intending to light it. With a savage glee and a mocking abandon, women and children displayed to the boisterous mob women's clothes on hangers and men's suits in a wide array of colors. From inside the palace, which had begun to burn, people rushed out, carrying Samsonite suitcases, expensive furnishings, carpets, silver dinnerware, porcelain cups and plates, and marble and crystal vases. Their faces were flush with elation, and the crowds lavished applause on them as they showed the bounty they had looted from the palace. Strangely, most of them immediately began destroying what they had taken, stepping on it, ripping it apart, or smashing it, to loud whistles of approval and hearty applause.

Leaving the scene of this mad circus, I felt impelled to find out what was happening to the rabbits. Outside their cages, the poor animals were struck with fear. A single person can frighten them, so just imagine their terror at being surrounded by thousands of enraged, agitated humans. The rabbits were scattering, desperate to escape from the forest of legs and hands. Shouts of glee and laughter at their desperate running only increased their terror, until they were paralyzed by it. The rabbits submitted to hands that started snatching them up and lifting them high over heads, along with slabs of various kinds of meat and bags of chicken and fish that had been plucked out of the refrigerators and freezers in the palace kitchens. Chants rang out, contrasting the hunger of "the masses" with the full bellies of "the masters." The rabbits turned their heads to look around them, their eyes blinking with astonishment and fear, as they floated over the sea of shouting mobs of people. After the rabbits had served as props for those who were leading the chants, they were put down again, only to be snatched into the hands of women from poor neighborhoods who had joined the demonstrations. They were dreaming of making a meal of *mulukhiyah* stew with rabbit, just like the kind that the governor obviously couldn't get enough of!

The authorities, who had evaporated into thin air during the day, solidified again in the cool of the evening. After the crowds of demonstrators emptied off the streets, the authorities gathered their forces, donned their uniforms, and sent out their olive green cars bristling with weapons, nightsticks, and officers who had regained their gravitas. They mobilized their informers, and began making arrests after midnight. My arrest was likely, but not certain, because I wasn't one of the leaders who had been lifted onto the shoulders of the masses so that thousands could call out and repeat their slogans. True, I was an opponent of the regime, but my role was limited to writing for student publications posted on campus bulletin boards and speaking at student conferences. In the protests, I was merely one individual in the crowds, too timid even to shout out slogans along with everyone else.

I stayed at home until 2:00 a.m., unable to fall asleep. My ribs, which had been bruised against the steel of the palace entrance gate during the day, began to ache painfully that night. I took some strong sedatives, but no sooner did the medicine begin to take effect than someone came to tell me that there was a massive police sweep making its way through the poor neighborhoods surrounding the old city square. The news surprised me, because that meant that they must be arresting thousands, but my informant went on to explain that they were only arresting people if they found one of the governor's rabbits in their houses, as evidence of theft and pillage. Perhaps they wanted to add a criminal charge to these arrests, to take them out of their political context, so they could smear people with the crimes of destruction of property and theft. Now that the pain in my chest had subsided I felt invigorated, and instead of lying down to sleep after the banging-up I had received earlier that day, I found myself putting on my clothes and getting into a fight with my parents, who tried to make me stay at home, fearing for my safety if I went out at that hour, breaking the curfew that had been announced on the radio and on television during the evening newscast. But I left anyway, and my feet quickly led me to the old square. I imagined that I would lie low in one of its corners, to observe those absurd police roundups, being careful not to come into contact with police informers or officers, who had spread out everywhere and were authorized to arrest anyone on the slightest suspicion. But after lurking for several minutes in one of the hidden corners of the square and seeing the looks of confusion on the informers and the soldiers, and on some people who had gathered here and there, where the streets opened up on to the square—all this made me leave my hiding spot and move closer to what was going on.

A heavy rain came down in buckets and then stopped a few minutes later, leaving the surface of the square glistening with moisture, the streetlights surrounded by a halo of mist. That's when the rabbits appeared, white and hesitant, emerging from the back streets. Quickly, whacks from the informers' canes sent them back into the streets again, as did agitated blows from the security soldiers' nightsticks, the raps of rifle butts, and the furious shouts of officers. The order they had been given was that rabbits had to stay inside the houses so their occupants could be arrested for involvement in a crime. After two citizens had been arrested this way, warnings flew like wildfire over the rooftops and through brittle walls made of drywall, tin sheets, and exposed brick. The word went out that the rabbits needed to be put outside quickly and banished from homes. The battle began with silence and caution on the part of the locals, and with brute force and zeal on the part of the security detachment. The former slipped the rabbits outside through slightly opened doors, shooing them away with a whisper. The latter blocked the rabbits' paths, driving them back with their clubs and rifle butts, and with kicks from their heavy boots. Then the skirmish turned into open defiance from the locals, as they sent their children out to remove the rabbits from their homes—for who could hold children responsible for anything? Then they helped the children's efforts by making a dreadful racket that terrified the rabbits, to drive them out of their streets in the direction of the square: whistling, pounding on doors and metal surfaces, banging pots and pans, clanging brass mortars and pestles, reverberating screams, and yells. Even volleys of *zaghareets* were launched from those ramshackle homes!

A great commotion flared up in the neighborhood, and it continued until dawn, as the security forces were unable to persuade a single rabbit to go back inside the house it had been in. The efforts made by the security forces to get the rabbits to return to the backstreets and into houses took on a savage character. It turned into a frenzy of heavy nightsticks, whacks from rifle butts against the asphalt, and kicks from infantry boots—all directly aimed at the heads and bodies of rabbits. Blood began to appear on small heads, long floppy ears, and white fur. At first, I observed what was happening with sardonic amusement at the ridiculous situation. But once blood began to stain the bright white fur I had held close to my chest that memorable day, my anger began to boil. I almost got myself arrested by the security forces that evening, but a hidden factor intervened to change the scene in a surprising way: it calmed me down, and calmed down the commotion, the noise, the whacks of the clubs, the rifle butts, the heavy shoes, the *zaghareets* and shouts. It froze all the platoons in place. As if out of nowhere, dawn appeared, intensified by the reflecting puddles on the square and wet streets. The morning's light was strong, and under that glare, everyone discovered that the rabbits had disappeared.

The officers and informers were convinced the rabbits had secretly sneaked back into the houses, but an aggressive, exacting, and thorough search that went on until midday didn't uncover a thing. The security men settled for arresting people who they found had a cooking dish suitable for *mulukhiyah* with rabbit among their pots and pans—and even some who didn't have one. As for me, I turned away at sunrise, feeling dizzy from lack of sleep and from the intensity of swirling and conflicting thoughts. As a precaution against being arrested, I didn't return home, but hid out at the home of relatives. Two days later, I was arrested as I was distributing leaflets demanding the release of my fellow students who had been apprehended.

Twenty-six years have passed, and I am returning to that same place at night, the old city square, in darkness more pitch black than it was on that night so long ago. I wait for an unusual apparition of white rabbits to show themselves in this inky blackness. Dozens of people have gathered in the open recesses around the square, waiting for the miracle. There are dozens more like them, whose faces I can see silhouetted on balconies and through windows looking out over the square, peering into the darkness. I now know some details about those rabbits, who were linked inextricably to that colorful part of my distant, cherished youth. They are of the Buskat albino variety, so in addition to their soft, abundant bright white fur, they are distinguished by their rapid growth, which makes them the size of small lambs by the time they are a few months old. Their eyes are like black cloves, and their movements are slow and fluid, like dragging, although when they need to, they can take long, high hops, and they can run very quickly for limited distances. There were ninety-eight of them in the rabbit coops in the palace. Three of them were found dead in the palace garden, and three others in the streets around the city square. Four cooked rabbits were seized in the homes of four poor families, two with *mulukhiyah* and two without. Two women were arrested as they passed by the Second Precinct police headquarters carrying rabbits on the afternoon of the day of the demonstrations. The police raids on Wednesday evening only netted two rabbits in two homes, all of whose occupants—including the children—were arrested.

As for the remaining eighty-four rabbits, presumably most of them were involved in the battle on the city square, which ended with their mysterious disappearance at dawn. A number of explanations were proposed as to why the rabbits vanished that day: that they had found gaps between the walls of dilapidated houses and dived into them; that they had fallen into an open sewer—or had let themselves fall on purpose, in order to flee humanity, either those humans who were shattering their bones with clubs, rifle butts, and heavy military boots, or those humans whose perennial state of hunger made them rush furiously to flay them alive and gobble them up before they were fully cooked. Then there were some unusual explanations that attributed it to something magical about those rabbits and their puzzling disappearance. And here it's been twenty-six years and the puzzle is still a puzzle. The square has undergone an ugly transformation as residential towers and office buildings in odd shapes and colors have grown thick around it. But what lies behind these towers still shows that some things have not changed, and in fact have reached critical proportions: the ramshackle houses—what's left of them—are still in their same places, although now further deteriorated. Those houses that were cleared away have returned to gather at the far edges of the city, in the form of straw huts and houses of mud and tin, inhabited by people whose chronic hunger harbors a readiness to skin rabbits alive and devour them raw. Twenty-six years were not enough to solve the riddle of these simple creatures and of an ugly fight that never ended. So would I find in the depths of this night a solution to the riddle that has lived with me and with this once-beautiful city for all this time?

Three o'clock came, pitch black, with a lifeless torpor. The square's asphalt was wet with a trace of the brief but heavy showers that occur this time of year. The puddles on the wet square didn't shine, because the darkness seemed total and all-encompassing. There was no moon in the sky, and no stars whose light twinkled in sought-after serenity. Along with many other people, I was waiting for the rabbits. And stealthily, stealthily, with no sudden movements, I saw—or thought I saw—white bits of shadow slip silently into the black ring of the city square, at the bases of houses and high buildings. They grew numerous, and gathered in groups, until the black of the square seemed speckled with their delicate wriggling white as they turned around this way and that. Even though my heart weighed heavily in my chest with weariness and exhaustion, I asked myself, hardly believing it, whether what I was seeing was real.

On an Elephant's Back

The elephant takes fright only via its sense
of sight, so take care if you use their backs
as lookouts, watchtowers, and observation
posts. The elephant can fight, strike, and
trample with his legs. The kings of Persia
frequently executed men by having them
trampled underfoot by an elephant trained
for that purpose.

—al-Jahiz, *The Book of Animals*

The elephant is a marvelous creature, and
symbolizes a thinker. Everything about it is
marvelous, and it is more prone to thinking
than any other animal.

—al-Jahiz, *On Mules*

When Tarquin Hall traveled to Assam in
northern India in 1998 to record the hunt of
a rogue elephant that had killed forty people,
he found that as a youngster the elephant had
been abused by an alcoholic owner and was
now enduring unbearable pain from a rusty
iron chain embedded in one leg.

—Cindy Engel, *Wild Health*
("Psychological Ills" chapter)

I've never known terror like the terror I endured on the back of that elephant climbing up to Fort Jaipur, even though I've had my fair share of terrifying moments in my life. They have been part and parcel of my travels, starting with my journeys as a young man sleeping rough on the roofs of trains. Travelers who are poor to the point of destitution stow themselves away up there, in the company of thieves, tramps, electric wires that can cut the necks of the unwary, and bridges that suddenly appear above their heads, ready to crush them if the roof-riders don't lie low, stretching out flat on their stomachs at just the right moment. After roughing it in my youth, there came travels in beat-up cars and run-down buses that brought me to the edges of cliffs in the Red Sea Mountains, gorges among Lebanon's mountains, and deadly crevices in the peaks of Tibet. I once flew over Laos' mountaintops in an ancient Russian plane with an engine on fire, and made my way through the rapids of the Zambezi River, its turns and its dangerous falls, in a worn-out canoe that never stopped bobbing above and under the water the whole trip—and I don't know how to swim. Walking on foot, I crossed the mined areas they call the killing fields in Cambodia, and floated in a hovercraft above the waters of Victoria Falls before they drop off far below. And for seven full years I did gymnastics professionally with one final goal: to turn myself into a circus trapeze artist, facing death with every leap on the flying trapeze

for the sake of executing an aerial backflip or two,
known as a reverse somersault.

I craved fear for reasons other than the ones psychia-
trists label "compensating acts" because, quite simply,
in coming face to face with terror, I tasted varieties of
pleasure and euphoria that you can't help seeking out
again and again once you've tried them. Repressed
physical sensations open up the pores of your every-
day existence to the hidden horizons of the universe,
the dazzling light that makes your eyes go wide, the
shudder of the skin shedding blood, the poundings
of your excited heart, and the warm glow that floods
through your spinal column to the center of your
brain . . . That preternatural alertness that comes to
life in your four limbs and spreads from there to your
whole body, the feeling that your ability is reaching
its climax at the same time as your terror. It's an
adrenaline high, according to scientific research done
on practitioners of extreme sports, such as skydivers,
mountain climbers, whitewater rafters, tightrope art-
ists who walk between skyscrapers, or climbers who
scale those same skyscrapers all the way to the top.

For the sake of that high—we'll call it an adrenaline high, as they call it—I cast myself into the jaws
of danger many times, choosing the most unsafe approach instead of what was safe and comfortable so
that I could get that high and feel its narcotic effects.

It made my travels more enjoyable and unforgettable. Usually, primitive and unsafe modes of transport are the best way to get somewhere unspoiled, off the beaten path, and hidden from view. By this logic, I preferred to climb up to Fort Jaipur on the back of an elephant, rather than by a car or a microbus outfitted with special tires. The elephant ride would take me up to the fort on a narrow, cramped, and steeply rising road that looked out directly over a terrifying drop, five hundred meters straight down, ending in a dry-lake basin crammed with boulders and rocks with deadly edges. On the other hand, mounting the back of the elephant would stimulate my imagination, evoking images and sensations of the maharajahs who built the fort atop this incline and lived there for generation upon generation, until they passed away and the lofty, formidable fortress was turned into a tourist destination and an object of marvel.

I knew that riding an elephant wasn't an entirely pleasant experience. It's true that towering over the world on top of a moving back that size, and at that elevation, is a wonderfully exciting experience, but one that is combined with body pains that can be withstood only by people who are used to riding these elephants—limber Asians with slight physiques, whose smooth skin and small joints indicate they have flexible bodies. After all, an elephant isn't a camel that rocks its rider backward and forward, in a way that aligns with the bending and straightening motions that follow the natural structure of the human body. And it isn't a horse that puts the rider into a prancing gait. Nor is it a donkey that jolts its rider. The elephant is a living mountain that moves on four solid legs. They swing forward with a deliberate heaviness and alternate their steps with no warning. The front right foot lifts along with the back left foot, to pound a giant step onto the ground, then the front left leg and the right back leg take the next giant step. With each massive footfall comes a painful rearrangement of human bodies as they cling to their places on the enormous back. The source of the pain is this wrenching motion, which occurs on a tilted, outstretched axis, not suited to the responses of a normal human body that has not grown accustomed to riding elephants since childhood. The massive, heavy steps cause the rider's joints to grind against each other like millstones, especially parts of the spine, then the pelvic bones, the clavicle, and shoulder joints. It was a painful experience I had embarked on before, on an island in the middle of the Mekong River near Vientiane and at a heritage preservation conference in Bangkok, but I had no hesitation about repeating the experience in Jaipur: I expected the pain, but I didn't expect the terror.

On the low slope where the road up to the fort began, there was an elephant "taxi stand" where the elephants lined up one behind the other next to a wall the height of a one-story building. It was like a raised platform with open balconies that led out to the elephants' tall backs. The elephants were painted with drawings of branches and flowers that went around their eyes and covered their foreheads, extending to their long trunks. The saddles on their backs, where the riders sat, resembled wide wrought-iron bedsteads. They were furnished with a great raised seating area and cushions that covered the wrought-iron handrail that surrounded it, at the height of about one foot, to protect riders from the likelihood of falling. The litters were secured horizontally by means of wide, thick leather belts. It seemed likely that the belts could only be elephant hide, wrapped around great wrinkled bellies the color of graphite.

Along with others making the ascent, I climbed the stone staircase leading to the top of the wall, where there were platforms from which we could proceed onto the litters on the elephants' backs. But our movement up the stairs seemed slower than it should have been, and I noticed there were a cluster of Indian policemen up there. I overheard bits of conversations around me about there being a detailed inspection that had to be done before we could be allowed to get on. These security measures were being taken as a precaution due to the situation in Kashmir, the sectarian clashes breaking out in Hyderabad, and train bombings in Mumbai. No problem, I said, precautions are necessary, and extremism is blind: it doesn't

distinguish between a train and an elephant, or between an enemy and bystanders, or between a person
and a rock. For extremists, the important thing is to
blow something up, even if they do their cause more
harm than good with their explosions. But when I
reached the top of the wall, it seemed wrong to me
that the inspection, after going through passengers'
bags and purses, as well as their clothes, moved on to
people's bare fingers, as the policemen grabbed people's hands and held them up to their eyes in the sunlight while inspecting them finger by finger. They did
the same thing with people's toes, after making them
sit down and take off their shoes and socks! I submitted grumpily to this inspection, and even after I took
my place in a corner of the saddle litter on the back of
one of the elephants, I couldn't rid myself of my feeling of disapproval, which turned into astonishment. I
was too distracted by my attempt at solving the riddle
of the fingers to notice that the elephant had started
moving uphill . . .

There were ten of us riding on the elephant's back,
not including the driver who sat in front near its head.
Among the ten there were four boys who couldn't
stop winking and joking with each other. As they
cleaned their fingernails with little pieces of straw,
they stuck the straw out front and below them to poke
the elephant. The driver turned to them and glared at
the pieces of straw. Then he looked angrily in their

direction and fumed with rage, talking rapidly in the local language, making what seemed to be a curse or a threat, or both. They behaved themselves for a few moments, then went back to laughing, winking, and mocking. With a questioning look and a hand gesture, I leaned toward one of the four boys beside me. There were traces of shyness and gentleness on him, despite the mischievous behavior he was up to with his three friends. In fact, the naughty look vanished from his smooth brown face. He seemed shy as he answered me in accented English: *aantsh.* For a moment, the word seemed cryptic, because I wasn't expecting his accent. Then an accompanying gesture from the boy, making dainty, minute, rapid movements with his fingers, flipped a switch in my confused brain. In astonishment and confusion, I blurted out, "Ant . . . ants?" Smiling shyly, the boy nodded, then we continued our whispering conversation, from which I learned that ants had become the latest tool of extremism, helping carry out terrorist operations in countries that use elephants as work animals for transportation, hauling, tourism, and festivities—in Laos, Cambodia, Myanmar, Thailand, Sri Lanka, Nepal, and India. No one knew when ants were first used in a terrorism operation, or where it was they became a threat, but warnings about this technique had struck the region like a continent-wide epidemic. There were numerous stories about incidents where elephants had flown into mad rages after ants had been inserted into their ears,

driving them insane. They rioted and crushed dozens of people under their heavy feet and demolished
houses, shops, cars, and gardens—doing more damage than any explosive charge in a booby-trapped car
or any roadside bomb could do.

Once the reality of this terror-by-ants had been
made clear to me—since several voices of those who
were on our elephant's back joined in to complete
the picture—I began to think about how the people
who were capable of such acts weren't all the same.
Whether it was ideology, religion, race, or politics,
opposition movements and armed hostilities in these
countries made up a wide spectrum of mutually in-
compatible kinds: agricultural and industrial barons
and drug lords in southern Laos and northern Thailand, Maoists in Nepal, the jade mafia in Myanmar,
incense-tree gangs in Cambodia, and various sepa-
ratists with religious and ethnic claims in Sri Lanka,
some Indonesian islands, and northern India. They
were divided by political and sectarian affiliations,
but they shared the ant in common when it came to
wrongdoing. Could it be that what they were doing
wasn't wrong? Can a wrong be used to right another
wrong? Was this a case of loss of perspective: our vision gone blurry and our blind spot come into focus? Is
a fire deliberately set to burn down houses capable of
selecting its victims? Does an explosive charge hidden

in a garbage can or in a car rigged with a detonator or under a train seat have eyes? Do ants have eyes when they are inserted into the dark porches of elephants' ears? Do they compensate for their blindness by biting the elaborate, sensitive nerve endings that are blocking their attempts to escape? With their fine, tapered mandibles they bite those exposed nerves, thus sending jolts of lightning into the brain of this massive eternal creature, causing him to explode in madness. He bursts into life and shakes the riders off his back, so that they tumble to the ground from high up, angrily flung off by an elephant filled with black rage. His massive body, weighing tons, moves quickly as he grinds under the millstones of his feet the people who have fallen off his back, as well as anyone who happens to find themselves nearby. He stumbles about, shaking his enormous head to drive away that thing snapping away deep in his nerves. He totters, slamming his sides against walls here and there, pulverizing those who happened to have sought refuge within them, thinking the walls would save them from the pandemonium of an elephant gone mad.

Suddenly, I was beset with terrifying images of different ways to die. I could be a victim of any one of them if our elephant's potential for violent rage was realized. I could fall off his back onto the rocks on the path leading up to the fort. My bones would be shattered, and his heavy, giant foot—or feet—would finish me

off, making mincemeat of me. I might be able to save
myself from falling off his back, but end up in a headlong fall toward the rock wall on the right. I steeled
myself for the possibility of being crushed to pieces
between the rock and the elephant's haunches. Or I
might fall far from him, and far from both the boulders on the path and the rocks to the right: instead I
would go on falling far below, toward the dry lake
bottom five hundred meters down, to be torn to pieces
on the deadly fanged edges of boulders, seared by the
burning Rajasthan sun. Thirst would only add to the
sun's fatal effects, thanks to the extended drought that
had lingered in the region for several long years.

As I sat on the elephant's back, I could only see the
image of my bloody death. We had made it two-thirds
of the way up; the elevation appeared terrifying, and
the basin of the dry lake yawned with horrors. I found
myself completely indisposed to enjoy the magnificent
view of our ascent, or to observe the white towers of
the fort up close and the purity of the broad, gray
plain beneath the familiar sky nearby. I was busy
keeping an eye on the people riding along with me
on the elephant's back: which of them is a criminal
concealing ants lodged between his fingers, or under
his fingernails, or in a corner of his pocket, as he lies
in wait for the right moment to release his ant—or
ants—into the elephant's ear, to make him burst into
madness here in this deadly spot? Afterward, the

criminal would have to find a way to escape at just the right moment, by hanging on somehow to let himself down quickly and stay out of the elephant's way as it went mad. Would he be happy about the bloody and destructive success he achieved by provoking the elephant into madness? Or would he feel an intoxicating rush at watching people fall and get crushed, their bodies torn to pieces on the rocks and sharp-toothed edges of boulders, or mangled and bleeding on this rocky road? There must be some kind of spontaneous high that these men are seeking, beyond whatever political opinions, religious creeds, or blood feuds they espouse. Is it a rush like the one I often felt when facing dangers? Another adrenaline high that makes them sow terror and provoke it without being hurt by it themselves? Their bodies are aroused, and they virtually float on air with wretched joy. Their bloody achievement fills their bodies with an extraordinary energy and alertness as images of bleeding human bodies gleam in their eyes; bodies they caused to be torn apart, impaled, or crushed. A shudder of lust ripples over their skin, while a frisson of secret pleasure convulses within them, revealed only by the sensual glimmer sparkling surreptitiously in their eyes.

I could only see myself trampled, mangled, or hurling down toward the sharp angles and edges of the boulders, whose sharpest blades and pointiest teeth were the parched heat and the burning sun. It seemed like the elephant was climbing up a slanted wall as he made his way up the last third of the road to the fort. Although the riders clung to their places by holding on to the iron barrier or by digging their fingers into the fabric of the thick cushions underneath them, the elephant's steep climb—once we saw his giant head appear, rising up in front of us—threw us all backward, and our ten bodies piled up in the back corner. There were excited screams and shouts of hilarity, but I was shouting only out of pure terror since I found myself being flung off, then sliding down the elephant's rump outside the iron railing. My fingers clutched desperately to the wrinkles of thick gray skin while my feet dangled in empty space. And with that miraculous agility that bursts out of nowhere in someone feeling terror, I managed to grab the elephant's tail and held tightly to it with both fists, which were working with an extreme subconscious precision. That allowed me to bring my body weight down to earth, as though I were sliding down a pole to the ground.

And by making mental calculations with the remarkable alertness that the terrified possess, when my feet were a half-meter or less away from the ground, my body recalled a distant memory of a gymnast making his body fly up using a rapid arch-swing motion that widened his swings to take him farther away from the trapeze bar or the edges of the parallel bars. I let go of the elephant's tail, while my body avoided the movement of the heavy pounding feet. I fell on my ankle at a distance and crouched, rolling over to lie flat on my back. Then, finally, I leaned on my side, and stared . . . The elephant continued his ascent, while the passengers on his back, who had turned around, looked in my direction with eyes widened in utter amazement!

She-Asses

In a dream, a female donkey represents a
woman destined for a life of abundant bless-
ings, offspring, and substantial income. And
someone who dreams of riding a female donkey with its foal behind it will marry a woman
who has a son. The Arabic word for "she-ass"
(*al-atan*) is derived from the verb "to come"
(*al-ityan*)—perhaps because her braying indi-
cates the approach of evil or ill tidings.

. . .

The young man who is given to weeping
and who drinks the milk of the she-ass leaves
off his weeping.

—al-Qazwini, *The Wonders
of Creation*

I have to remember as I go back over everything; perhaps I'll understand what happened. That day I woke
up from an afternoon nap—something I am never
in the habit of doing—in a stupor, as though I were
drunk. That may have been due to the effort I had ex-
pended that morning sending my wife and children off
to spend vacation at their grandmother's house, and

also because of the surprising peace and quiet which descended over the apartment once I was alone in it. I made myself a cup of mint tea, having woken up from my nap with a hankering for it, mixing up some tea with mint and sugar. As soon as I sat down to rest on one of the armchairs in the living room and lifted the cup of tea to my mouth, I was startled by the intercom next to the apartment door. It gave an alarming buzz, as though a dozen times shriller and more insistent than usual. I stood up and the first sip from the hot cup spilled onto my hand; some landed on the shiny, light-colored floor tiles between my feet. I pulled myself together, barely keeping the cup from falling out of my burned hand, and set it down in exasperation on the small table beside the armchair. Then I hurried over to silence the terrible intercom. I lifted the receiver in annoyance, and shouted as I had never done before to the doorman on duty in the lobby:

"What is it, Husayn?!"

"A guest coming up to see you, doctor."

"Wait, what guest? What's his name?"

Normally, I don't ask for details like this, and I don't raise my voice like I did this time. I just calmly say, "Send him up, please," because in no more than a minute I will find out anyway who is coming up. That's the amount of time the elevator takes to reach the third floor, where my apartment is. I caught Husayn, who was a decent fellow, by surprise. He seemed completely taken aback, since he didn't say a word.

Instead of his reply, I heard a loud, short squawk, and a strange voice reached my ears:

"I beg your pardon. You don't know me, but I know you. I know all about you. I'm coming up to see you."

Normally, I am easily irritated when faced with rude behavior, to the point of doing something stupid, and my preferred response in a situation like this would at the very least be to pour out a stream of invective on the head of this uninvited guest at a time like this. But instead of the shower of vitriol I should have unleashed on the owner of the strange voice over the intercom, I found *myself* taking a cold shower, one that was invisible, soundless, effective, and mysteriously affecting: it nailed me in place, and kept me frozen there with the intercom receiver in my right ear. Without hearing the sound of the buzzer, or a knock on the door, I found myself moving like a sleepwalker: I put the receiver back in its place and opened the door to the visitor.

For a moment, I felt fear, since outside the door to the apartment there was only the darkness of the hallway and the glimmer of the elevator's light at the far end, confirming that the visitor had come up. I couldn't see him at first. Where could he have gone? I thought he was playing a joke on me, and had stepped back onto the staircase beside the door to confuse me a little.

I was furious at the possibility that he would joke around like this, but for the second time, my burst of anger vanished, and I found myself, in that moment of distraction, meekly saying in greeting from a great distance:

"Please come in . . . please come in."

Instead of the visitor approaching from the corner near the stairs, I found him standing right in front of me. It was as though he had emanated from the darkness, or as if someone had pressed the staircase light switch at that moment and I noticed him. But then I remembered that the staircase light had been broken for a while; some of the residents had put off paying their share to buy new equipment, and the old equipment hadn't been repaired.

There was something unusual that I sensed about the strange visitor, as though a specter of extremely dim blue light was gently touching his pale skin. It made me look around for the source emitting or reflecting this light from somewhere in the sitting room, where I invited him in. There was no light source that was giving off this blue color; in fact, to be precise, nothing in there had any blue in it. I certainly had never laid eyes on this man before he showed up at my apartment. I definitely hadn't run across him anywhere where he had left the slightest impression on my memory. He was a stranger I was seeing for the first time in my life. But in spite of that, he seemed to know me well, and to know my apartment, too, since he looked at ease and sat down in a relaxed manner, evincing no curiosity, like someone who was already familiar with the place and its owner. I was fidgety, confused, and distracted. When a look of anxiety flickered for a moment on his face, I imagined that maybe I could place him from somewhere, from a place that was vanishing from my memory. But he put an end to that possibility by surprising me with a quiet peremptory statement that sounded like an order:

"You are wanted."

I thought that explained things: he had come to recruit me for one of the security services. I felt confident about that, since he was giving off clouds of mystery that set my imagination spinning, so much so that in my mind's eye I was seeing him enveloped in a tinge of nonexistent blue light. I wasn't afraid of being recruited by some government agency, since I was inclined (as everyone who knew me in the last few years was well aware) to have no interest—an almost absolute lack of interest—in the world of humanity. My interest was fully engaged in the animal world. My inclination was not to bother anyone, and this way of thinking made me relax in front of my visitor. I was about to begin provoking him with a joking question, which would suss out which agency he had come to recruit me for, but he stunned me with a surprising statement, as though he were reading my mind:

"You are wanted because of your interest in animal behavior."

The extremely dim blue glow once again touched the man's forehead, and I noticed his facial features, which indicated Mediterranean roots: a wide forehead; firm skin; eyes that showed a mix of blue, green, and brown; and hair that was curly, despite its fineness and light color. His features suggested a congenial nature, as if the man were originally from Alexandria, but those same features were surrounded by an invisible field of authority and aloofness. As soon as I started thinking about arguing with him—that I was no scientist, merely an amateur scholar whose curiosity was piqued by animal behaviors—he stunned me again:

"Your explanation for why the presence of African elephants is so important, and the way you traced the tragedy of the Himalayan bear, and your discrediting of widespread ideas about ostrich behavior—all these and more corroborate that you are wanted now."

I stood up in front of him, perplexed, although I had surrendered completely, following where he wanted me to go: my two works about the African elephant and the Himalayan bear were published, so anyone could cite them. The topic of ostrich behavior was completely astonishing, because I had barely begun to write the first line of it, which didn't yet convey much of anything, and I hadn't talked to anyone about its general outlines, including this notion of "discrediting widespread ideas."

❧

Before I could sit down again, he got up and walked in a circle around the room, heading toward the apartment door, while I walked behind him. When his face and gimlet eyes were not directly in front of me, a disturbing thought dawned on me: it was possible that I was being set up for some scam, and I should arm myself with something for self-defense, if I were to face an attack. I thought about quickly picking up a knife from the kitchen and hiding it under my clothes without him letting him see me, but I was afraid I might arouse his suspicions by making a move that would attract his attention, and which I wouldn't be able to explain away. Then, too, I couldn't imagine stabbing anyone with anything, even in self-defense. I found a plausible alternative directly in my path: one of those canes that I like to acquire from different places in the world, which I hang here and there on the walls of my home. This one was the Burmese one, made from compact, solid teak wood. It had been polished and ringed with inlaid copper Asian decorations that added to its solid heft. It was as if it were calling to me: *Pick me up*. Making a short, fast leap, I grabbed it, and all of a sudden, the man I was following turned back to me with a sudden, expressionless glance. Then, as he continued walking, leading me outside, he repeated:

"Good. Maybe you'll find it useful."

We walked away from my building, with him leading the way, even though I seemed to be walking next to him. I imagined that he had a car he had parked nearby, but that idea disappeared after we had walked for some distance, and he—with me behind him—turned off onto al-Saluli Street in the direction of Murad Street. I was in my house clothes, wearing a pair of slippers. My hair was mostly a mess, like someone who had just woken up. In spite of that, I wasn't troubled by any feeling of embarrassment while I walked down the street looking that way. I wasn't self-conscious. Instead, I was filled with dread, as he led me with determined strides somewhere I didn't know. His choice of al-Saluli Street heading toward Murad led me to expect he would hail a taxi going to Giza Square, or would take the overpass onto Abbas Bridge to the other side of Cairo. But his strides didn't change their rhythm when we reached Murad Street, where there is no break in the flow of car traffic. He began to cut across the insanely busy street, and I followed him—terrified at first, then utterly dumbfounded after two or three steps. The flow of cars stopped completely, as if by a hidden traffic light, and a safe path opened up before us to the sidewalk on the opposite side of the street. Cars piled up, halted in place, without a sound. Nor did they make a sound when they started moving again behind us. Silence seemed perfectly logical as we made our way along quiet Kafur Street. Its peace and quiet were still maintained by private security teams. Although there aren't many of them now, they haven't left their positions stationed around the house of the man whose

assassination didn't put an end to security personnel
around the walls, since his wife was still living there.
What *did* change was that you could now look directly at the house, since the tragic death of the owner
did away with the imposing power that used to radiate
from its high white walls, while the crowns of regal
date palms in his garden, the curtains of revealing
white lace behind the window panes, and the abundant flowers in the ornamented balconies remained
just as they were, and so too the trim gray tower at
the top of the house. In the heavy silence was a loud
emptiness and a gloomy feeling of abandonment, despite the house being radiant and white as sugar. It
gleamed in the remaining light of day as we passed
by. I pictured that lady who remained by herself in
that vast expanse of loneliness; I pictured the fleeting
nature of power, and the withering away of life. She
was a beautiful, white-skinned lady, and her beauty
multiplied her broad influence. I noticed a shadow
moving behind one of the curtains. My eyes stayed
with the shadow and I began to walk backward, but I
snapped out of it and found the man I was following
had gotten ahead of me. He had already taken me
past Nile Street, and led me along the riverfront sidewalk towards the Yacht Club entrance. He started
heading down the stone steps just as I was catching
up with him. He turned left and went up the small
wooden bridge attached to the terrace of the floating restaurant. There was no one there to stop him.
The place seemed empty of its employees and guests,

who flock there in great numbers at a time like this. He descended from the back end of the terrace, and I descended after him, onto a moving dock toward a medium-sized launch with its lights on. The launch pulled away, smoothly cutting its path between the numerous motorboats and yachts on the Nile waters in this spot around the club restaurant. If not for the light shudder as it set out, you wouldn't have known the motor was on: it launched without any noise—in fact, without a sound—onto the broad open waters of the Nile, while I sat on a seat in a small, rundown lounge belowdecks, not saying a word.

The water, throbbing and rippling with the movement of the motorboat under way, could be seen up close through the glass of the two portholes of the small lounge. Cairo carried its head high above the water, crowded with buildings, residential towers, tall hotels, and bridges. I couldn't see the east bank of the Nile, which we were heading toward. Everything I saw was located on the west bank, which we were leaving. Was that due to the design of the boat's portholes? I wanted to ask the man who had led me here, but he wasn't there. I remembered he had left the lounge for some matter that required his presence on deck, but now he was gone. He had been gone a long time, or so I thought, when I noticed that blazing orange streak, the reflection of the setting sun, descending on the water. Then the streak began to fragment and gradually die out, until it suddenly vanished, and I discovered that night had fallen on the waters of the river. The black waves twinkled, reflecting the light of distant lamps, or stars. Then the sparkling lights on the water began to blaze up quickly, until I imagined they were reflecting thousands of torches on the shore, which I now realized were approaching. I felt fear, then terror, and my heart was pounding. My throat was burning from a dryness I wasn't expecting; it seemed to me that the boat was cutting a path through a river of fire. I stood up in alarm, but no sooner did I call out to the man who had brought me than I was surprised to find him there, even before my voice left my mouth. He stood at the top of the stairs that went up to the deck from the belowdecks lounge and called to me:

"We're here . . . Come on up."

I actually used my cane to support myself, since I was suffering from a serious exhaustion that only revealed itself once I started moving. The exhaustion combined with dizziness, the kind that might come over someone after a long flight across the ocean or over an entire continent. But this fatigue fell away at the sight of the water, which was either on fire or was reflecting a blazing conflagration. I saw it through the two portholes of the small lounge. With my right hand, I reached out to grip the polished wood of the banister on the small staircase, while poking the stairs with the tip of my cane—in my left hand— to support me as I went up. I went up the few stairs with both feet and both hands, in fact. It seemed to have taken me the time it would take to climb the steps of a tall tower. I paused at the top of the stairs to catch my breath. The purple reflection of the fire, flickering on my companion's face, scared me. It flickered on my hand and on the columns and ceiling of the covered terrace on deck. I gazed across the wide open expanses and saw something I couldn't believe: a riverbank of undulating hills where voracious fires blazed, lighting up all the hills in a terrifying all-encompassing conflagration.

"No, no . . . This isn't Cairo!" I shouted in terror.

I turned away with a vigor that had now spread through my body and violently grabbed my companion, shaking him by the shoulders and shouting in his face:

"Where am I? Where are we?"

To my astonishment, the man felt as light and brittle as a hollow doll, and in his face, on which the lights of the fires flickered, I read the deepest sorrow and grief that could come over a human face. Then his beard went white and grew long, and his hair went white, too, as if he'd become an old man in a matter of moments. He didn't speak, and I didn't speak. I didn't want to ask anything else of him because I found that a sense of certainty was floating untethered in my head, as if a program had started running in my mind and was displaying bits of data on my brain: "This can only be Rome as it burns. This is the River Tiber, which cuts through its hilly landscape and continues to the sea. And this is the Palatine, the largest of its seven hills, on which the ancient village once sat. And here it is in flames that are engulfing the poor neighborhood at its foot. The flames are spreading, descending on all the low-lying districts below the hills, then ascending, lusting after the city's high points. Rome is being burned in its Great Fire, and it is now 64 AD, but where is Nero?" As the question occurred to me, suddenly I was circling in the sky over the city; its black night combined with the blackness of the ashes of its fires and its illuminated tongues of flame. I moved away, drifting in the direction of one of the hills of Rome, as if I were in an invisible space capsule, or plunging into the depths of a scene in 3-D. My invisible capsule hung beside a balcony from which a misshapen, mentally deranged man looked down. Although he was wearing an emperor's garments, his stomach was big, his legs were small and knobby, and his head was excessively large. He was pointing at the city burning below him, jubilant and greatly elated. With his pudgy right index finger, he followed something—or some things—moving. Then he laughed madly, and through his laughter, kept repeating:

"The scene . . . O God, what a scene! A marvelous scene!"

He repeatedly pointed at something, following it with his finger, without stopping his laughter, so I looked for a long while at where he was pointing, following with my eyes the direction of his finger. I discovered lit torches rushing by like crude shooting stars that refused to die out. They set fire to something in one place and ignited other fires elsewhere; they entered fires and came out of them at faster speeds and with larger flames. They passed through new conflagrations, only to ignite even newer ones, but who were they, these fire-starters, whose transgressions Nero was finding so uproarious?

"This is what you came to observe."

I heard the voice of my companion answer the question that had come to me without my having to utter it. The voice came from my right, so I turned, but I couldn't see him. I had no capacity for further fear and bewilderment, so I didn't dwell long on hearing this voice spoken by an invisible figure. I found myself looking closely at the flying torches crossing back and forth across Rome's great and terrifying fire. I was getting closer and closer as I examined them, until I could see what they were, and shouted in astonishment:

"They're burning donkeys!"

There were hundreds of them, running blind and terrified in their panic. They ran into fresh fires that burned them further, fires that blinded them and increased their terror, making them run faster and spread the conflagration.

I moved in closer and discovered that all these donkeys were female—she-asses with full udders. In fact, their udders were so full, they were congested, and their pent-up milk poured out of them as they raced about, extinguishing narrow strips from which steam rose where the milk came in contact with the flame. Before long, the steam evaporated and the traces of extinguished fire closed over as the flame burned over them again, and in fact, burned further, while the living torches moved back and forth, and Rome continued to burn. Where did all these she-asses come from?

The question flashed in my mind, and instantly the answer came, from my right:

"They originally belonged to Agrippina, his mother. Most of them belong to his mistress, Sabina. The rest belong to the wives and mistresses of the men in his retinue."

The combination of the two names, of Nero's mother, Agrippina, and his mistress, Sabina Poppaea, had the effect of an explosion lighting up my brain, and my memory began to go to work, as if it were receiving a signal from remote depths. I saw the imperial escort of Sabina Poppaea as she traveled among cities ruled by the man whose heart she had won. In the middle of her retinue walked a herd of five hundred she-asses who always accompanied her. Every morning, Sabina would bathe in jugsful of the fresh, warm milk of these she-asses. Their milk was an elixir for her skin, restoring its seductive vitality and charm, and bestowing on it a freshness and softness that beguiled Nero to the core. It was an exchange: a narcissistic woman gained some influence over male tyranny, while some of the woman's whims, stirred up in her by nature, made their way into a narcissistic man. Each side was eager to downplay this exchange, and thus the woman's skin grew more delicate, and the man grew crueler in his tyranny. Does this not partly explain Nero's madness and brutality, after his liaison with Sabina Poppaea, who made him seize her by force from her husband, himself a friend of Nero's? Later, Nero killed his own wife, Octavia, and his teacher, Seneca, and slaughtered thousands of people before butchering Sabina Poppaea with his own sword!

"His mother, too?"

The voice came, again from my right, but I didn't turn toward it, since I found the horrible scene taking shape before me: after Nero had kicked his mother, Agrippina, and raised his sword over her, she threw herself down at his feet and screamed at him in a frenzied anguish:

"Come then . . . split open the womb that bore the beast!"

He did not hesitate to obey her shouted command, and he fell upon her with his sword, repeatedly bringing it down on her in a frenzy, hacking at her and spilling her blood, jumping back only when the lacerated corpse had ceased making the slightest movement, as if it were an enormous serpent whose malicious bite he didn't trust even as it was dying. As though she were a snake that had not quenched its thirst for the domination she had never stopped striving for by toying with men. She betrayed Nero's father, a consul, in order to marry the emperor, and tricked the emperor so that her young son would inherit power. After her son grew up and became emperor, when he wanted to put an end to her domination, she plotted against him, so that he might be deposed by the emperor's legitimate son, whom she had deposed previously.

Agrippina went, and Sabina came, inheriting from her the she-asses she had left behind. Sabina increased their number, until there were five hundred of them, and all the concubines imitated her. Keeping she-asses became a popular occupation in Nero's Rome, and their stables were spread out in the lower-class district where their grooms lived. The fire broke out, and the she-asses burned. Their fear of fire induced an excess of milk in their udders, which become swollen, adding a new source of pain to the one caused by the fire. The burning she-asses were in a frenzy as they fled from fire to fire, their bodies become torches that ignited other things, as the conflagration swept through Rome.

"Oh God, what a marvelous scene!"

I could no longer hear the madman's voice, but his cackling outburst echoed resoundingly within me, and I realized that his infatuation was focused on the points where the blazing torches were located, as they traced purple outlines with their movements, collided, intersected, and ran parallel with each other, against a background of orange tongues of flame, ash-gray smoke, and the coal-black rubble of homes. Nero believed himself to be an illustrious poet, and his final words, some years later when he took his own life by stabbing himself with his sword, were:

"How great an artist the world will lose with my death!"

Was it likely, if his mother hadn't pushed him to rule, that Nero would have proven to be a poet or an artist or even merely a sensitive human being? Did his escape from his mother's snare save him from his mistress' trap?

"You have seen and understood. So what do you say?"

I heard the voice of my companion again. I thought that if I turned to him I wouldn't see him, but there he was on my right, while I saw Rome in flames gradually recede. I realized that we had returned to the open waters of the river. There was nothing I could say in response, so I said nothing, and remained in my silent state even after I returned to the small cabin within the boat. I saw the reflected lights of the fires die out and melt into the darkness of the water and the night. I realized that the waters of the Tiber were receding, while the waters of the Nile were approaching. Against the darkness of the river's wavelets gleamed the lights of that fountain in the middle of the river, the lights of the residential towers, the hotels, the floating restaurants, and the bridges. I turned to my companion to say, with emotion:

"Cairo."

"You know the way."

That was his response, before he went up to the boat's deck, and I had a feeling I wouldn't see him again.

White Bears/Black Bears

From all appearances it would seem that the bears are enjoying the sunset, taking pleasure in the aesthetic experience. Scientists laugh at the naïveté of this interpretation. How could a bear be capable of aesthetic appreciation, a contemplative state? Some aesthetes also believe other people are incapable of such a state . . .

. . .

One can doubtless go too far with this, listening, for example, to a bear exhaling and claiming that he is sighing with melancholy awareness of the transience of things, observing his world and thinking that one day he will no longer be present to witness such beauty—an ursine Rilke.
— Jeffrey Moussaieff Masson
and Susan McCarthy, *When Elephants Weep*

The village was on low ground at a level below the road, and my eye was caught by those black bears tied to trees in its central square, beside the mud huts with straw roofs that were typical of the houses in this village. It looked like it was abandoned, but for a stray woman who stood there, following us with her eyes after we parked our car and got out. No sooner had we planted ourselves on the village soil than the huts began to cough up their inhabitants, heading in our direction. The woman remained standing where she was, outside a circle of dozens of standing bears rocking back and forth, their trainers banging on tambourines, seminaked children, goats, and dogs—this circle that surrounded us like a thick fence of animals and humanity.

"Fifty rupee, mister . . . Ten rupee, mister . . . Ten rupee . . . Ten rupee." Dozens of thin, scrawny hands stretched out toward us, and dozens of black eyes and worn-out bodies reached up to us insistently and imploringly—the hands and eyes of both children and adults equally, asking for a gift from the "tourists" who had set foot in the village, since its inhabitants were accustomed to taking their bears to the tourists, even to the farthest point in Rajasthan.

It was a strange scene: black bears sitting upright on their hind legs, some of whom had begun dancing that sad, loping dance they do; dozens of trainers holding the ropes tied around the bears' necks, while big tambourines shook to the beats of the trainers' fingers; the din of the rhythm of the tambourines; the voices begging for something; and the pounding of dozens of bare feet on dried cinchona leaves crackling on the ground. It was a ring of noise and clamor, and in the middle of it all, not a sound escaped from the submissive bears, nor from that lone, skinny woman, who retreated to a far corner, looking at us and the cluster around us with resigned annoyance. She spat in our direction and in the direction of the circle of people while muttering under her breath, or at least making a sound I was unable to make out without getting closer to her. When I broke through the group to head toward her, the circle turned pear-shaped, with her at its tip, while voices around me clamored, "Leave her alone, mister . . . leave her alone . . . she's crazy, mister . . . Crazy . . . Crazy about the bears."

"Crazy about the bears"—the designation struck my mind like a bolt of lightning, and I set about shoo-ing away the bears, the trainers, and the crowd from around me, until I ended up directly in front of the woman. She looked around thirty years old, although madness and misery had ruined her good looks. Judg-ing by the traces that remained, she must have been dazzlingly beautiful, and when I approached her, she didn't shy away, nor did she leave off her muttering or her expressions of displeasure. Although I had made an effort to quiet down those gathered around me, I shouted with all the anger I had in me, gesturing and yelling in English, "*Quiet! Quiet! Shut your mouths!*" and the only Hindi word I knew: "*Bas. Bas. Bas.*" It was as if I were aiming magic rays at their faces, shooting them out of my eyes as I shouted. Their faces froze, their mouths closed, and a rare moment of si-lence occurred, during which I became certain that the woman was in fact muttering something, but without making a sound. She was babbling incomprehensible, unspoken words. I thought it was likely they were insults and hate-filled curses for the people she saw, and perhaps for life as a whole. When it seemed to everyone that my attempt to communicate with her ended in failure, the noise went back to its previous level, gradually at first, before reaching a climax that made it impossible to distinguish any individual sound. But I managed to hear a voice that started off with, "She mingles with the bears at night . . . You'll get nothing out of her, sir . . . She's crazy." I looked around at the similar-looking weathered faces that were near my own. I tried to pick out who had said the words that caught my attention, but the noisy concert blotted out any possibility of accomplishing anything along those lines. Without planning to, I began to repeat in a kind of yell: "She is crazy . . . She mingles with the bears at night . . . She mingles with the bears at night!" I happened to turn toward a man who nodded to me, confirming the truth of those words. I pulled the man by his wrist, bringing his ear up to my mouth, and I began talking to him, shouting out questions: "The woman mingles with the bears at night?" He nodded yes in response. "Do you know her story?" He nodded again, then I leaned up to his ear and in a stage whisper asked him to go to our car parked on the road and wait for us there.

☙

"I swear . . . she mingles with the bears at night . . . You can confirm it yourself. I will be your guide so you can see it. I will only take one hundred rupees from you. The bears are dangerous at night, and you must have someone with you who knows how to command them. I will be your escort. I won't take more than one hundred rupees from you. All right—only seventy-five rupees. You will see her as she associates with the bears."

The bear trainer I had chosen had preceded me to the car, accompanied by his bear, and he made this offer. It was more than I was expecting, but he came down in his price, until he had reduced it to only ten rupees! I wasn't bargaining with him on my end; in fact, I didn't believe him, and I tried to brush aside the unbelievable idea he was putting forward, as well as his promise of adventure under cover of darkness in the bear trainers' village. The only thing I wanted from him was the story he might have to offer about a madwoman who was widely known to be intimate with bears at night. But with his intense entreaties and pleading, he pushed me toward an encounter I hadn't been expecting. I knew my curiosity couldn't resist his modest but exciting offer, especially since it only suggested tantalizing threads of the woman's story without filling it in. Thus, his offer that I go with him at night to the village below the road, with its straw huts and dozens of bears tied to tree trunks, and then the woman coming out onto the scene of her supposed madness in the dark—all of this made up an experience whose allure was difficult to resist. Despite the warnings of my Indian companion, Bayram, about the likely consequences of this adventure—that one of the bears might attack me, or the madwoman might give me away and wake up the people of the village, who would gang up together in the dark in a way that was very different from how they acted in daylight, becoming aggressive and malicious like nocturnal animals—I wasn't dissuaded; instead, I was drawn by an irresistible magic thread to take a chance on observing something exceptional. The bears didn't frighten me: they were tied up, with their claws and teeth pulled out, as I had seen when they were among their trainers, or in the shade of the trees whose trunks they were tied to.

I made an agreement with the man that we would meet at midnight, without his bear coming along, in Fatehpur Sikri, at the foot of the vast staircase leading to the ghost city's lofty entrance gate. At the time, we were heading to Agra from Jaipur and would be returning along the road we had passed before. The only place near the bear trainers' village that I was familiar with was Fatehpur Sikri, which I felt sure the man could get to in ten minutes on foot, the same time it would take us to get there from Agra. From there, we would set out to the village together. We would park the car on the road, go down the slope plunged in darkness, and observe the woman who

was crazy about the bears as she made her appearance and carried out her awaited performance, that
exceptional performance, for only ten rupees!

During the day, we drove past Fatehpur Sikri, and
we passed it again at night on our return. The first
time, we got out of the car and made a tour of its
vast, deserted ruins—perhaps the largest and strang-
est ghost city in the world. At night it seemed to stand
out in the darkness in all its ghostliness, and despite
my preoccupation with the supposed story of the
woman who was mad for bears, the story of Fatehpur
Sikri continued to sink its claws into my mind: one
of the vast cities of the Mughals who ruled India for
three centuries, following the Mongols' destructive
arrival from Central Asia. A city planned by the Mughal emperor Akbar to be a new, matchless capital
for his rule; an imperial city made entirely of dark
red sandstone in its palaces, its reception halls, its
towers, its barracks, its shops, its prisons, its cemeteries, and its great mosque. Akbar put all the grandeur
and skill of Mughal architecture into this city, but for
some unknown reason, it was abandoned. They say
it was due to its high altitude, its canals being only
intermittently filled with water. Did Akbar think that
water would defy the law of gravity in deference to
his imperial command and ascend to the summits of
his remote city above the peaks of mountains? The
water didn't rise, and Akbar's stronghold became a
ghost city: the wind whistles now between its towers and monkeys roam inside it, descendants of the

monkeys that the emperor had acquired and that continued to reproduce, growing in numbers there down
to our own day. The city's space is an open domain
of endless intersections for the flittering bats that nest
in the tops of arches of lofty stone gates, in the pinna-
cles of fort towers, and in the eaves of roofs. Even the
spontaneous swarms of wild beehives in the hollow
spaces of the high-up ornamentations seemed like
gloomy blotches to me, as though they were yet more
empty bats' nests, despite the valuable wild honey
gathered by inhabitants of the villages surrounding
this fortress-city.

Something always weighed down on my heart
whenever I stood in the courtyards of the Mughals'
forts, in their palaces, in their cemeteries that resemble both forts and palaces, and in all the vastness of
Mughal gardens that have coursing water channels,
marvelous fountains, polished stones, and marble inlaid with precious and semiprecious colored stones
that magnificently trace enchanting flowers and radiant, marvelous designs. None of it could lift the
mysterious black vise from my heart. It maintained
its grip as long as I was among the ruins of the Mughals in India. Even in the presence of those elements
appealing to racial brotherhood and religious tolerance, manifested in the blend of architectural styles
and sculptures, it could not loosen this mysterious
grip from my heart. Even Akbar—the most famous
Mughal emperor, the one who most promoted brotherhood and tolerance—perennially took the shape of

an oppressive, grasping phantom, despite the echoes of his greatness in the ruins of places and across the pages of time. I couldn't erase from my mind the flavor of conquest that tarnished the story I had heard about the friendship that arose between the Indian rulers of Rajasthan and the emperor who let them rule in their capital of Jaipur. He didn't attack or oppress them, and they gave him one of their daughters as a wife. To him, she became the most beloved of all his numerous wives and countless concubines. I never found that love story believable. I can imagine the delightful sensations that flooded the Indian princess with rivers of desire, beauty, and Mughal fantasy. I can imagine the carnal fantasia that inspired the dark-colored drawings of the provocative and beautiful Mughal book of desire, the *Kama Sutra*. But I cannot imagine a crack of daylight penetrating the darkness and gloom in the heart of the princess who had been given to the emperor when she was alone by herself in the final part of the night, or when that final part of the night was alone with her.

Like black upon black, the phantoms of Fatehpur Sikri, which means "the city of the great conqueror," continued to haunt my thoughts, casting their heavy shadows on images of the story of the woman who was crazy for bears. It heightened my desire to observe the spectacle that marked her peculiar character as I headed to her dark performance under cover of night.

In India, they have a remarkable method of hunting bears and taming them to make them servants obedient to the hands, spoken commands, and tambourine rhythms of their trainers, these skinny, barefoot, half-naked men. It is a long journey that the black bears make, all the way from the mountain peaks of Tibet, among the summits of the Himalayas, as they leave behind their freedom in the wilderness to submit to being tied up to trees in front of straw huts inhabited by the poorest of India's poor, in that isolated village in a low ravine beneath the road.

Bears love women! I used to think bears were content to love wild honey and were mad for gulping down testicles and salmon, as I learned during my time in Russia. In India, they discovered bears' love for girls, and they have turned this love into a lure, since hunters rely on releasing a dazzlingly beautiful young woman into the bears' grazing lands, in spots where they have previously laid a skillfully camouflaged trap on the ground. As the woman passes along a designated path, the hunters hide in the treetops, concealing themselves with thick branches, cocking their rifles to be fully prepared to fire, while others hold the ends of the ropes of the trap in their hands. The hunters hold their breath; the woman's breathing quickens. When one of the bears appears, he follows her like a human adolescent—desirous, confused, and distracted. He follows her, slowing down his pace; with head bowed, he can barely see anything other than her in front of him. He loses all his cautiousness, and stumbles in his steps, while she is eager not to stumble despite her excessive fear. She crosses over the trap, over a safe pathway which she knows about and which she has practiced crossing over before. As she is moving past the opening of the trap, the bear is directly positioned over the pit. Then the ropes are drawn tight from the treetops, the bear falls in, and the woman breathes a sigh of relief.

The bear is tangled in the snare's rope, and the men tie it up further. Right away they set about pulling out its sharp teeth and claws with a pair of iron pliers, until its snout and chest are stained with blood. In the bear trainers' village, the training begins once the injuries caused by pulling out its teeth and claws have healed, and the bear is turned into a beaten child or a broken old man: he has no way to obtain his food by himself, so someone has to hand it to him. His food is like that of small children or the very old: crumbs of bread in milk or water sweetened with sugar, each bite given for obeying a command; each time he disobeys a command, food is withheld. There are various commands: he has to stand upright like a human on his two hind legs, shake his head to the beat of tambourines, or dance to the same beat with his full weight.

The deadly black bear of the Himalayas is turned into an object of ridicule, one that is painful to behold when you look closely at the details. The bear's toothless snout appears floppy, like a worn-out rag, and its paws, with the claws pulled out, swing about like feeble, unkempt brooms. The massive body that rises up to stand, then rocks back and forth to the swaying beat of the tambourines before the bear handler, reveals the humiliating contrast. As for the eyes, oh those small eyes on the verge of tears! Even though the scene is designed to evoke mirth in the eyes of spectators, there is something about it that kills off any enjoyment for anyone who looks carefully, even if only for a moment. Thus I would often see spectators pay the bear handlers without following the bears' dance closely and then quickly look away and leave. So I was amazed when the man claimed that this woman mingled with the bears, even if only in the dark.

The day they led her from the far south to the mountains of the north to be bait for a bear, she was softskinned and charming, with a free and lithe physique, smooth golden-brown skin, and wide, honey-colored eyes. Even though she was wearing an ornate, shining silver engagement ring through her nose, she was not yet married. Her husband-to-be, who had given her the nose ring, was a bear handler, young like her. But he was wiry, skinny, and nervous, and was among the group of bear hunters. They loaded their rifles and settled in after readying the trap during the day, in a patch of the Sikkim Forest. It was biting cold despite the time of year, which was the height of summer. They coached the woman several times about the plan to catch the bear, then lit a fire to drive away leopards and wolves, and alternated between sleeping and standing guard in turns until daylight came. As for her, they set aside a space for her in the corner of the tent and let her sleep. But mostly she didn't sleep. Was it out of fear of what the next day would bring? Or was it from the warm prickling sensation like ants crawling over her feverish body as she lay there surrounded by the bodies of men, including her husband? Or from both? No one knows, but she didn't sleep that night, as witnesses related, their testimonies piecing the story together. Perhaps she dozed a little at the end of the night, since the men saw her face looking radiant in the morning, and her spirits were high. Then the ritual of the bear hunt began.

Rifles in hand, the men climbed to the tops of trees, tracing a wide circle around the hunting site, and they signaled to the woman that she should sing flirtatiously and sway back and forth. No know knows whether it is really a woman's singing voice, her flirtatiousness, or her feminine fragrance that calls to a bear from afar to make him approach her. From their hidden perches, the men watched the mass of coal-dark velvety blackness cut through the dense green thickets toward the source of the swaying and singing, and when the bear entered the circle, one of them threw a small, light pebble at the woman's feet, telling her to start moving. She stopped singing, started walking, and the bear followed behind her. The towering forest muffled the sound of her breaths, and there was only the sound of the woman's feet treading on piles of leaves on the forest floor, and the sound of the bear's steps as he followed behind her, at one moment lowering his head, then the next moment looking up at her with his small eyes, glassy with desire. A profound silence descended on the forest, and the sound of the woman's breathing—unhurried in spite of the accelerating terror in her veins—was clearly audible. The sound of the bear's excited breathing was clear, a few steps—no more than several meters—before the pit trap, but to the men crouching motionlessly in the high treetops it seemed infinite, and to the woman it seemed as though it would never end. It was the dangerous interval between the bear falling into the trap and falling onto his prey. At that moment, the men raised their rifles and set their sights on the bear's head as a precaution against danger, although the danger had already occurred: the terrified woman's feet stumbled on a dry branch that was concealed between piles of leaves on the ground. She stumbled when she tried to look behind her because her fear was so intense. At the same time, she tried to keep herself from turning around.

The young woman fell flat on the ground, with her face turned toward the bear. The bear stopped moving the instant she fell. Her eyes and the bear's exchanged glances: she saw only a giant, motionless, coal-black bear, sitting up on his legs; he saw only a vulnerable woman cast down on the ground at his feet. The breathing of the woman and the bear quickened across this slight distance separating them, while the men on the surrounding trees held their breath.

It was only natural that this tableau would freeze time in a situation like this, as though the woman were frozen with fear and the bear were a human adolescent freezing up when an opportunity is suddenly flung open before him and he can't believe it's really happening. In that motionless instant, the men shifted their positions in their lofty hiding places in order to fire from several directions at the bear's head so they could take him down instantly, before he could reach his victim and match the sharpness of his teeth and claws with the intensity of his burning desire.

But this time was an exception.

In the brief instant after he stopped, the bear took two smooth, quick steps, and the woman was in his embrace. The men with the rifles couldn't get

a clear shot from above the treetops since the bear—
who must not have been an adolescent, but was sex-
ually mature enough to be impulsive—immediately
stretched out flat on his side after putting all four
limbs around the startled woman. She ended up with
her head lying on his shoulder like a pillow, as though
he were being careful about pressing on her with his
full weight so as not to hurt her. Firing at the bear's
head was impossible without risking getting the
woman killed, either from a bullet striking her head
that was touching the bear's, or from the bear's teeth
and claws, if the first shot didn't kill him instantly.

That was the moment the guns froze.

If we were to measure the length of that moment by what took place within it, it would be ex-
ceedingly long—beyond what the mind can conceive.
The woman, who had been transformed by fear into
a block of ice in the bear's embrace, must have had
enough time for the ice to melt. It had to have melted
despite her ongoing fear, because she stopped screaming and calmed her thrashing. Her breaths came one
after another, until the eyes in the treetops could see
her heaving chest and the unrestrained, wild body
heat that enclosed the woman's body. The torrential
flood of physicality was not a side effect of an impas-
sioned animal nature, but was animal nature itself,
the essence of brute desires. This animal nature found
for itself a torrid spot in the dense, overgrown jungle
of the human psyche. It seems that just as this steamy
part of the jungle in the woman's psyche was on the

verge of actually igniting, the sound of bullets rang out.

The bullets rang out, then, at the peak moment of their comingling.

A moment of passionate tenderness and, at the same time, of fear embraced by this tenderness. Then came the rifle shots, not to rupture that comingling, but to fix it in place.

They say that the bullets, in their white-hot trajectory, grazed the woman's face, causing an abrasion that left a scar like burn marks. At the same time, three bullets sank into the bear's neck, jawbone, and head.

The bear didn't die right away, and the usual reaction in a situation like this would be for him to sink his claws and teeth into the nearest flesh. The woman's flesh was nearer to him than his own, but in a scene out of a storybook, he opened up his limbs as widely as possible and rolled over slowly to release the woman, without a single claw scratching her. He moaned as he lay dying with a sorrowful rattle in his throat, as if he were saying farewell to the woman, who had been struck senseless.

She remained in a catatonic state for forty days, during which she didn't speak to anyone, didn't move, and didn't eat except when they forced her to, by opening her mouth and pouring in milk, which was the only thing she subsisted on. Throughout those forty days she remained motionless and passive, like a wax statue, until her stiffness relaxed and then became fixed in that delirious, distracted manner of hers that I had seen in the bear trainers' village that morning—and as it would be that evening, when we went to see her after midnight.

Did trepidation dilate my pupils? Or was the brilliance of the countless stars in the purple Rajasthan night sufficient to illuminate the scene with a thin silver light?

Accompanied by the bear trainer and my driver, Bayram, I crept into the low depression of the village, now sunk in sleep. I seemed to be in a strange dream, framed by a glimmer of light, phantom creatures, and shadows. Ghostly huts and ghostly cinchona trees where the night breeze whispered . . . I didn't see the bears at first, since they were fast asleep, their black color part of the earth's blackness, masses of black against black. They would hardly have been visible to me if not for a feeble twitching by one or another of them as they slept.

We hid ourselves behind a hut that the bear trainer led us to and waited. It seemed to me that we waited a long time: perhaps it was the thirst of anticipation that made me feel that time was passing slowly. I poked the bear trainer standing beside me. "Are you playing a joke on us?" I asked him.

"I swear, she comes out at night," he answered, lowering his voice and emphasizing the words. Perhaps it was my strange surrender to the breeze that night that quelled my curiosity. The silence, the shadows, the slight drop in temperature, and the translucent darkness: all this soothed my sense of anticipation, until I almost closed my eyes and fell asleep standing up . . . The moment I lost my desire to watch her, the woman appeared, like a shadowy being that came out at night and roamed about, or so it seemed to me. Very cautiously, we began to follow this shadow, and the masses of darkness began to stand up, as though a secret signal had passed through the peacefully sleeping bears, and they stood upright in response. Now the movement had reached the village square—dozens of bears tied to the stumps of trees were standing up like humans, and the apparition we were following began to pass by them. I could make out that she was carrying a bucket, which she was barely able to lift. The only noise was the sound of light footsteps on the dusty ground. Then I could make out the woman's whispered—in fact, affectionate—voice. Whenever she approached one of the bears, she said something to it, stroked it, and talked to it in a soft voice, as if it were a child being given favors. With her hand, she scooped out some of what was in the bucket and fed it to the bear, who impatiently and audibly devoured what she'd given it. Then she said good-bye to the bear with another pat before moving on to another one.

"She calls the bears by people's names . . . People's names she calls them."

The bear trainer leaned over to whisper in my ear until I could smell his terrible breath. I couldn't help but ask him a pressing question I had: "What is it she's feeding them?" My voice was louder than it should have been, and it caught the woman's attention. Perhaps she had good night vision, being so often accustomed to moving about in darkness like this, because she noticed us and was instantly agitated. She yelled something, then began shooing us away, throwing a splash of something moist at us as we ran away from her. I thought it was mud she had picked up off the ground as she chased after us, screaming.

We had to get away from the village; our car, which we had left on the road nearby, was our place of refuge. We stayed inside this iron sanctuary, hearing the woman, who had stopped at the foot of the road, yell at us. Then numerous apparitions began to emerge from the huts, moving in the darkness in the direction of the screaming woman: the village had woken up and was coming outside. In an instant, it looked to me like the anger of an irritated crowd that we had roused from their careworn sleep, even if the likely source of its anger was protected by the cover of night.

After we had gotten a sufficient distance away from the village, I felt safe, and I noticed the sticky liquid the woman had thrown at us as she chased us away. One splash had struck the right side of my face, and a little of it had made its way into my mouth. It was bread soaked in water sweetened with sugar. So that was what she was scooping out of the bucket and feeding to the bears. And that is what got me thinking about her disturbed mental system, which was organized only in this particular aspect: arranging all the necessities for her nighttime forays; collecting the bread, water, and sugar; soaking the bread in the river until it became soft and moist; then arranging to go out regularly after midnight. The rhythm of an organized daily life, albeit in reverse. It must have become an internal rhythm for her, a kind of inversion of many of the rhythms within her. I thought about that when we passed by Fatehpur Sikri again, when voices reached us from beyond the great gate, as though a game were taking place in the ancient courtyard there. In my memory there flashed a remarkable image from a short-lived historical period that made me think of this game, but I was afraid and tired, and didn't want to stop to find out the source of the sounds coming from the ghost city plunged in darkness. Our car drove past the darkness of Fatehpur Sikri. The farther the car got from the city, the closer that remarkable image from a vanished era came to my mind. The Mughal emperor Akbar used to play chess on a gigantic chessboard, with squares made of black jasper and white marble, the size of the courtyard in front of the palace. The pawns were the beautiful slave girls who filled his palace, and he and his opponent would move them with the point of a finger directed from the imperial balcony. He would move them, naked in diaphanous black-and-white gowns—an image that stuck to my imagination and didn't leave me until I entered the liminal space that exists between waking and sleep. How strange that, when sleep came over me, I saw a game of chess in a fleeting dream: the pawns, on a gigantic chessboard in the open space of a great plaza, consisted of bears—white bears and black bears shifting places in fixed moves, without a trace of any players.

The Elephants Go to Drink

> Birds such as pigeons can hear the low-
> frequency sounds known as infrasound;
> elephants share this ability, and use these
> sounds for communication.
> —John Downer, *Supersense:*
> *Perception in the Animal World*

A lion headed out to hunt, and met with
an elephant, who fought him viciously.
Overmatched, the lion escaped, with blood
flowing—for the elephant had wounded him
with his tusks, so he was unable to seek his
prey. And so for days the wolf, the crow, and
jackal had nothing to live on from the lion's
leavings.
> —al-Muqaffa', *Kalīla wa Dimna*

Has the lion ever killed an elephant? And
when has he ever eaten it?! Aside from that,
even if he were to, the elephant might give
him a kick—either killing him, or sending
him fleeing somewhere else.
> —al-Jahiz, *The Book of Animals*

When an elephant falls on his side, he is
unable to get up, so the elephants let each
other know about it. A big elephant comes to

152

him and places his trunk beneath him, and
the rest of the elephants assist him until the
fallen elephant is up on his feet.
                    —al-Qazwini, *The Wonders*
                         of Creation

As he welcomed me and my photographer colleague
into his office perched high on one of Windhoek's
hills, the president of the University of Namibia, with
an air of friendly graciousness, said to us apologeti-
cally, "I believe you're the first delegation to inquire
about the wealth of wildlife in our country. Not just
from your Arab countries, but from anywhere in the
whole wide world, including the many European
countries. I am not the only one who is interested in
your arrival; in fact, all concerned parties in the nation are, but we are at the beginning stage of nonrac-
ist rule and are staggering under the weight of this
severe economic crisis, which certain people are fu-
eling in order to embarrass the new regime. They are
putting pressure on us to make us resort to violence.
We are strongly opposed to violence, but we are on
our guard against it. We'll provide you with one of
the university's sturdy cars, along with one of our
staff, who will be both driver and guide. We'll work
to smooth the way for your assignment, and reduce
your expenses to the extent that we can for all the
places you're going."

At the end of the meeting the university president phoned his secretary. While we were standing there exchanging our final courtesies and taking photos to mark the occasion, a tall young man with delicate features and build knocked on the door and entered. The university president gestured to him with affection. "And here is Katisha," he said. "He'll be accompanying you on your grand tour." I could immediately sense his affable spirit in that clean, brightly lit place, ornamented with colorful and charming touches. But of course I couldn't imagine that that spirit would turn into a gnawing enigma and grief over the disappearance of someone close to you—or rather, someone who became close to you—in uncharted wild country.

The office of the university president was spacious, with white walls on which hung colorful paintings with warm, serene African designs. The simple furniture was black and shiny, while the fabric on the seats repeated the same warm, serene colors of the paintings. Like the university president, Katisha was Black—that light black coloring with delicate features that characterized most of the people of Africa's south, suggesting the validity of the theory that the people in these regions are descended from ancient emigrations from the East African coast, since they look so much like the people of Eritrea and Somalia—in fact, the resemblance is quite strong. They even resemble Nubians in Egypt. Perhaps that was the secret reason I felt at ease with them from the first moment I was among them. But their easygoing manner was no simple matter, and in fact it encompassed complex dimensions of the country's makeup, which has absorbed the unique qualities of the different terrains that surround it: the Kalahari Desert from the east, the Atlantic Ocean from the west, and the depths of the African jungle from the north and south. All these lifeworlds mingle and move about through the country's heart, with a precise, elegant Prussian touch that was left behind by German colonial rule and retained by the white residents, who in this country became Africanized more than anywhere else in all of Africa's south. That Germanic touch was maintained with acumen and political organization by the fighters of the South West Africa People's Organization front that finally came to power following the departure of the racist regime.

The university president suggested we go to the coast by way of the mountains to the west, then head to Etosha National Park so we could photograph lions and from there return to the capital on the eastern highway. That way, we could come into contact with different varieties of Namibia's natural life. For four full hours I sat in the Land Rover with Katisha at the wheel, cutting a path through the labyrinth of orange-red canyons and ascending the dry clay hills and mountains, rippled with colors ranging across pink, brown, and ivory—eternal topographies permeated with mystery that put us in the uncharted reaches of the universe, although we were still here on earth.

There was no other guide we could latch onto to keep us safe other than Katisha, laconic behind the driver's wheel. He only spoke when we asked him something, which we did only a few times, when the car emerged from deep within the uncharted desert onto an exposed surface that showed a few signs of life—a small highland oasis, cultivated land beside the road, or a pasturage for livestock that we passed by, its primitive gates made of tree trunks set between upright boulders. When we set off down a level road that ran beside spacious ostrich farms, Katisha spoke without being asked. "There are no more mountains," he told us. "We're approaching the coast." He didn't seem happy about that and lapsed back into silence. On the smooth, emptied-out road that ran directly to the coast, we discovered that the fear that had settled on our chests during the long trek through the mountains stayed with us. Then we saw the ocean, and what an ocean! It was the Atlantic, with the expanse of its vast bosom and its endless horizons and its violent, pounding surf, although the waves washed up gently on that tranquil African beach. Its captivating call enticed me to move from the back seat to sit up front next to Katisha. I noticed that he seemed to be experiencing stifled shivers with every beat of the ocean's waves. I began to observe the natural world from two perspectives at once: I saw everything as it was around us, and I saw Katisha's very private interaction with all this reality. We passed through ostrich farms, prompting the giant birds to run alongside us with extraordinary speed, and I saw Katisha nod his head up and down as if he were following along with the ostrich's gallop. We traveled along the coast road near the sea bird protectorate. Hundreds of flamingos flapped their wings as they rose into the air, revealing the ruby-red undersides of their wings and the coal-black feather tips bordering the red. I noticed Katisha's shoulders tense up as if they were sprouting hidden wings that longed to soar.

Our journey along the coast coincided with the celebration of the independence of Walvis Bay, which had been subject to the authority of the racist regime in neighboring South Africa. There were humble posters celebrating the occasion, and I asked Katisha about the place. He told me it was a few minutes away, and I nearly jumped with enthusiasm at this surprising news, and asked him to head there immediately. In fact, we got there a few minutes later, as the celebration was about to get under way in a bare-bones football stadium. Tens of thousands of Black Namibians were there, old and young, men and women, filling the stadium's stands and field. They surrounded the podium on which stood some ministers, leaders of the new regime, and guests from Mandela's party. There were also some white Africans who had resisted the former regime's racist and colonialist policies. The citizens and their leaders were wearing the best clothes they owned, a tumult of cheerful colors. But the clothes couldn't hide just how threadbare they were. Even the podium, seats, and loudspeakers were humble as well. But the overflowing joy eclipsed the rundown state of things, with Namibian flags flapping on poles and in people's hands, and with hurrahs and songs and that charming dance performed at African public demonstrations. I found myself extremely moved by this national innocence and political purity, even if I couldn't keep asking myself how long that national innocence and political purity would last when faced with the temptations of power armed with the force of a regular army and the allures of command bristling with the prestige of official authority. I was amazed to find that Katisha had no particular reaction to the rhythms of the celebration, like the ones he had with the running ostriches, the soaring flamingoes, and the ocean's roar. Yes, he was happy, but not so happy that it led to that feeling inside him that made his shoulders shake with a flutter, or made him tip his head to the side as he hummed along. More than anything, he seemed concerned that we not get lost amid the crowds, and that we hurry if we wanted to catch sight of the beach with seals at Swakopmund before the end of the day.

After ten full hours that had begun at six in the morning in the capital and ended with us depositing our bags in the rooms we had taken at the Europa Hotel, with its refined and spotless beauty that sparkled in the heart of Swakopmund, Katisha struck up a conversation with us for the first time, urging us to hurry to the seals' beach: "It's four o'clock now, and there's only a little daylight left." As the Land Rover made its way through the streets of Swakopmund, which looked like an enchanting bauble washed by the waters of the Atlantic, Katisha was not as eager as we were to be dazzled by the beauty of the buildings that dated back to the nineteenth century and that were painted with light, gay colors—pink, turquoise, ivory, lemon yellow, and sky blue. He didn't notice the radiance of the small gardens on the shore. With all his being, he seemed focused on the destination the car was hurrying toward.

A warm, light rain poured down on the coast. We took our time walking over the giant, smooth black boulders that led down to the sands where the seals gathered—hundreds of wet, dark brown seals on the damp sand, their round heads and barrel-like bodies gleaming. We skidded and stumbled, and Katisha moved from boulder to boulder with a slow, plodding step that didn't match his slender frame, clearly afraid of the waves slapping on the beach. With squinting eyes, he continued to follow them intensely with every slap. As we stood amid the crowds of seals, I saw Katisha's wet face dripping with compassion as he observed these plump, peaceable animals around him. There was an amazing congruence that linked his black eyes to the round black eyes of the seals, which seemed extremely human and childlike. It made me recall the tragedy these creatures suffer, with redoubled sorrow and anger at the wealthy men and women who are to blame for the slaughterhouses that condemn this species of God's creatures to death.

For these women's coats, special exquisite bullets made of silver are fired at close range in order to fell these creatures without damaging the valuable pelt and skin. For these old men's voracious appetites, the male seals' genitals are cut off and dried, then ground up. The powder is then added to the dishes of these rich old men, greedy to restore their lost virility. I noticed that Katisha's eyes glistened with a light moisture, as if the images I was thinking of were passing before his eyes, too, and I asked him, "So, have they stopped killing them?"

"They are still killing them," he answered, with a slow sorrowful shake of his head.

We spent the evening in Swakopmund. We needed to head to Etosha early in the morning, but our stroll around the small, marvelously pleasant city; that Germanic hotel overflowing with flowers; the dinner crowned with broiled lobster, selected from the glass tank containing live fish; that music that matched the candlelight everywhere; and the refinement of the charming young women of the hotel, with their various skin colors representing the city's mixed roots—it all led us to extend our stay for an additional day. Katisha wasn't happy about that. It is true that he continued to be an agreeable companion at all times, but he also never stopped chiding us for losing a day to what he called "superfluous stuff," and at dawn the following day, we set out on Katisha's advice to Etosha, "so we can see the animals when they are active before midday."

The two-and-a-half-hour drive didn't feel like a burden since Katisha was driving in a carefree mood, while from the car's tape deck came pop music with an African beat. Along the road, which cut through the countryside, followed a succession of peaceable villages and hamlets, full of color. When we passed the gate of Etosha National Park, I noticed that Katisha seemed to be flying. It was the first time we saw a herd of gazelle startled by the sound of the car. The herd fled, leaping across the road in front of us—leaps of astonishing height and beauty, one after another, which formed a magnificent living arc out of the gazelles' graceful bodies as they flew over the asphalt, connecting the two grasslands on either side of the road. Katisha immediately slowed down the car, and I saw him look at the arc of gazelles with the indulgence and affection of someone watching small children play, but instead of saying something about the gazelles, I found him muttering softly: "There are a lot of elephants here . . . They are big . . . Very big."

We stayed in two of the "bungalow" huts in the fenced-in area of the Etosha preserve known as "the campground." They were cabins built to resemble the huts of the tribes of southern Africa—cylindrical with conic roofs of thick straw—but their interiors were entirely modern, like deluxe hotel rooms: air-conditioned, with refrigerators and elegant bathrooms with running hot and cold water. Katisha was by himself in a single-person hut, while I and my colleague the photographer stayed in a two-person hut.

Katisha had fetched the car so that, when we came out, he could take us on a tour of the open parkland beyond the enclosed area. It seemed as though he had found himself at last; he seemed more animated and responsive, and allowed himself to be away from us for some time so that he could wander about freely in the wild country during the times we were resting. At our table in the campground restaurant, we noticed that he no longer adjusted to our eating habits by ordering common dishes like macaroni and filet of steak and potatoes. Instead, he ordered Namibian dishes whose names we didn't know, and told us that he had two names: one was a formal Christian name; the other was an African name that his own tribe used for him. The name Katisha was part of his tribal name, which he preferred to be called by. When he smiled, he revealed splendidly symmetrical, radiantly white teeth.

During the three days we spent in Etosha, Katisha would eat breakfast before we did and then would go get the Land Rover ready and fill it with fuel from the station attached to the campground. Just as we were finishing the last sips of tea, he would stand over us to get us to come out with him to the car. We passed through the tall back gate of the campground and left the four-meter-tall barbed-wire fence behind us, only to find ourselves deep in the savanna, heading into Africa's wild open country. At first, we would usually encounter gazelles, which would either flee from our path or, if we were at a distance, observe us with a simultaneous collective head turn by the entire herd. Then groups of zebras would appear; they were often near the gazelle herds, or were mingled with them as they grazed in tranquility and silence. Only rarely would one of them let out the faint sound they made, like the whinnying of a baby foal. It made us laugh because of the incongruity of the sound with the size of the wild zebras and the strength that stood out against the fascinating stripes on their hides. As we pushed on into the wild, giraffes began to appear, their heads high above the trees that concealed their bodies. Katisha refused when we prodded him to get close to them and rev the car's motor in order to drive them away so that we could see them fully. Instead, he took us to a remote area where we saw giraffes without getting close. They appeared haughty with their spotted bodies and their long necks in the middle of the savanna, as though they were floating high above the grass. At a dense thicket of trees in the forest, Katisha stopped and pointed up above. We saw the largest nests imaginable, belonging to weaver birds, and we caught sight of an actual attempt at predation undertaken by a snake going after some small birds, but we didn't want to stop at small predators like this; we were looking for the big ones: lions, cheetahs, and crocodiles. Katisha wasn't concerned with that; he was always going on about elephants: "We will have to see an elephant . . . African elephants are very big . . . They're enormous . . . giant . . . Even lions are afraid of them."

Despite the wide, flat expanse of wild country, the savanna's low elevation, the scarce trees, and the vast amount of land withered away by drought, Etosha continued to seem enchanting and cosmic over the course of our tireless tours: it never ceased to pull surprises out of its wild African bag of tricks. A herd of water buffalo, numbering in the thousands, darted in front of us. To our eyes, it was a black flood amid a storm cloud of deep red southern African dust, a flash flood before which even predators and ponderous herds of rhinoceroses fled in alarm. It was a wild sweeping onslaught that couldn't see what was in front of it or around it, but could smell the scent of water from twenty miles away. The water may be in a neighboring country, like Botswana or Angola, but the thirsty herd recognizes no borders and doesn't care about them. As much as Etosha revealed surprises, it remained cunning, hiding curiosities that were difficult to conceal, like the lions we were looking for, and the elephants that Katisha kept dreaming of.

At noon on the third day, from a distance of two hundred meters, we saw a pride of lions sleeping peacefully in the shade of some nearby trees. We couldn't get close to them, since Katisha made clear he wasn't keen on that, on the pretext that we could be exposed to danger by being in an open-top car, no matter how sturdy and high it was. "Those animals aren't safe," he said. "And up close, they smell terrible!" My colleague had to content himself with taking shots using the zoom lens. I followed the lions with a small pair of binoculars from the gear bag. I was amazed by the serene indolence, bordering on apathy, of these creatures as they rested on their savanna thrones. When I saw them, they were halfway between slumbering and lolling on their stomachs and flanks, in what resembled a collective nap. The only one of them that was up and about was a lioness among the cubs that were play fighting, while she roughly pawed at them whenever they got close to her. The big lion was lying in repose, and I couldn't make out whether he was asleep or awake because the binoculars I was peering through weren't all that strong, and they couldn't give me a detailed look at the lion's eyes. But he seemed dignified with his look of great sagacity and his alarming appearance.

"The leader is drowsy," I said, as I peered through the binoculars, and I heard my photographer colleague laugh out loud. Katisha didn't laugh, but I smiled as I thought about what they say about the big lion: that he makes himself feared and respected over a wide area, up to a hundred square miles, and that he sleeps twenty hours a day to make up for the energy he spends digesting the fresh kills he devours, which the lioness presents to him.

By sunset on the fourth day we still hadn't seen a single elephant. Katisha had been tirelessly looking for them, and it seemed as though he was looking for nothing else, even if only in silence. We had no luck with them, except in coming across spoor that always gave evidence of their having departed the place we had reached: mounds of their dung resembling great lumps of rock, or piles of giant bones and skulls— each one the size of a man. We got out of the car, amazed, to touch the skulls and bones, but Katisha just stood in front of them for a long time without touching them. Deeply moved, he told us that the place was an elephants' graveyard. Then he bowed his head for a long while as he muttered or babbled, making faint sounds that made us feel a sense of awe.

"What's the use of African elephants?" The question seemed petty when it was asked at a Friends of Wildlife Conservation conference I had attended in Pretoria nine months before my trip to Namibia. When I tried to answer it, I was at a loss, as were many others besides me. My uncertainty continued to pop its head up and expand in Etosha, perhaps under the influence of the notion that gripped Katisha. Touching the giant bones in the elephants' graveyard made me think about the moral aspect of the existence of a creature the size of the African elephant, reckoned to be the largest creature that walks the face of the earth. *Even lions are afraid of them.* This sentence, which Katisha had repeated in his continual stream of chatter about elephants, reverberated in my mind. While we were returning from Etosha at sunset on the fourth day, in the sublime red of the twilight that descended over the park as it reached its deepest moments of silence, I felt that perhaps I was grasping the essence of the answer: it is true that lions are afraid of elephants; in fact, I know that lions stay out of elephants' way, out of fear of encountering them. And I've never read or heard about a single instance in which lions went hunting in the presence of elephants. Here, then, is the crux of the matter:

Elephants frighten lions, and lions frighten whatever crosses their path, so the greatest source of fear in the wild is represented by elephants, a source of fear that doesn't prey on any animal and doesn't eat any animal's flesh. Do elephants play the role of a peaceful deterrent or of conscience against the temptation to use force by the arrogant beasts of the jungle? Does their presence represent an ultimate defense that protects the circle of life from enduring what would likely be bloodthirsty savagery, should predatory force—by its very nature—overstep the boundaries of what it needs to live and to safeguard its domain? Questions arose within me in the gathering dusk of sunset as we headed back toward the campground. For the first time, I felt the depth of Katisha's yearnings for elephants, and I wished it was day so that we could return and make every effort to look for these eternal creatures, so humble that their ultimate delight in quieting their hunger is to shake carob trees to make the pods fall down so they can enjoy them as a tasty meal. That's why some people accuse elephants of being responsible for the near-extinction of this species of tree, but these pods break apart as they pass through the elephants' innards, so that seeds come out of them. Some of these seeds aren't digested, but their hulls are softened and their centers become moist, and when they emerge with the elephants' dung, they are fully ready to send up new shoots. The plentiful natural fertilizer around them allows them to grow rapidly and sink their roots deep in the earth of the African wild. It is as though when an elephant destroys a tree, it plants dozens in return. Such is its life. And its death offers a lavish feast for predators and carnivores, which find enough to satisfy them in its giant body. It also keeps them from harming weaker creatures for a long time; a marvelous peace settles over the wilderness, as though it is paying its respects to the elephant with a great mourning period of gentleness befitting the strength of the elephant's own gentleness. I find it baffling now that some people cut off the tusks of this giant creature merely because it is the source of decorative ivory or gaudy trinkets!

Some time had to pass until I realized that seeing an African elephant—an African one, specifically—is no simple matter. Those elephants we see enslaved in the circus, or in cumbersome tasks of carrying and pulling things in South and East Asia, are not African elephants. The African elephant can't be domesticated, and when they are abducted and forced into a life of captivity in zoos, they become depressed and often die of that depression. Or they continue to live but stop reproducing in captivity.

"He will come here," Katisha said as we were having dinner in the campground restaurant. I turned to ask him to explain what he meant. "The elephant will come," he replied. He was using *elephant* in the singular, but he meant the plural, even though his English was reasonably good. I nodded my head in agreement, going along with him, but he insisted on clarifying what he meant, word by word: "The. Elephant. Will. Come. Here." I agreed with him, noticing his heightened emotion and the tension that made his long elegant fingers tremble. I thanked God that our days in Etosha were coming to an end, since it had been decided that we would depart the next morning.

We were tired after spending the whole day in the wild, without having anything to eat or drink except what little we had brought with us in the car. We were focused on collecting the greatest number of photos and observations about life on the African savanna in Etosha, from its awakening in the early morning until it settled down to rest—not to sleep, since the savanna doesn't sleep, but until its diurnal half retires and its nocturnal half—night-hunting carnivores, including the lions that had piqued our curiosity, awakens. We were only able to get shots of the lions lying quietly in the shade of the trees during the day. We weren't equipped with night-vision goggles and cameras, and besides, we didn't have protective equipment. We had worked for twelve hours without a break, so we turned in for the night directly after dinner. It wasn't yet eight o'clock. We left Katisha to go to his hut, and I went with my photographer colleague to ours. In a matter of minutes, we were fast asleep, still fully dressed in the clothes we had worn in the wild. How many hours did we sleep? About three hours, and then we woke up, startled by the sound of wild pounding of the door. It was Katisha in a state of joyous excitement who was hurrying us up, shouting: "Hey! Hey! He's here! I swear . . . I swear . . . He's here!" We had no choice but to follow him.

Katisha led us northwest, toward a corner of the campground we weren't familiar with. Many of the park's visitors were pouring out in the same direction, talking about the elephants. I turned to my colleague. "Apparently, there's something there," I said, and he lifted up his camera. As a professional photographer, he never went anywhere without it. At the far corner we found a semicircular stone wall, as wide as a Roman amphitheater, surrounded by stone seats. The people sitting on the seats were leaning over the wall, as though looking down from a balcony. At the same time, the whole place was covered with tall powerful floodlights, the kind used to light up stadiums at night. The silence seemed complete, and a number of park rangers were there in their khaki and light brown uniforms, greeting people as they came, warning them in barely audible whispers not to make a sound, "so as not to frighten the animals." As soon as we took our places on a long bench in the middle of the wall, we looked down on the surprising scene below: there was a large watering hole opening onto the savanna that lay hidden behind a dense grove of trees and tall grass. The lights reached as far as the eye could see, revealing a convoy of gray-black backs, enormous and convex, that swayed with a confident bulk as they approached the watering hole. Moments later, the grove burst open to reveal the first massive head, trunk, and tusks, and the first elephant in the herd made its full appearance. I turned to look for Katisha, and found him standing at a distance, indifferent to us and everything else around him. He brought his hands together to his chest as he followed the elephants' approach.

It was a giant live performance that had me so absorbed I forgot all about Katisha, and forgot all about my colleague, who must have forgotten about me, too. He was leaning over and running around without making a sound, moving from place to place, in order to take photos from different angles. The elephant matriarch appeared first in this nocturnal procession, then the young mothers, followed by their young, and at the rear came the males. Whenever an individual, male or female, arrived, he or she turned toward the elephant matriarch, so that their heads came near each other. Then they moved apart, while raising their trunks as though they were exchanging greetings. The matriarch's body turned like a giant living compass, steadily and slowly, and the other elephant's body turned in parallel, until the matriarch stopped turning at a certain point, and the other elephant headed in that direction to take the place she designated for him or her at the water's edge. The scene repeated itself until all the elephants were distributed around the watering hole. For the young, their place was beside their mothers, up front and center, while the males were on the sides. Without a sound, the matriarch slowly approached the water and waved her trunk over it. We heard the sound of massive blasts of air, which she used to clean the surface of the water, then she dipped her trunk in it to drink. After she quenched her thirst, she backed up a little, then tossed her trunk up high and let out a ringing blast. What was she saying? No one knew, but the young mothers, following her lead, repeated her actions: they blew on the surface of the water to clean it and didn't rush to take a drink themselves, but let their young drink first. If a young elephant continued to play with the water after drinking, he got a slap of the trunk from his mother, decisive and gentle, which stopped him and sent him back behind her. Then the mothers and young withdrew to the rear, so that the fathers and other males could come forward at last. They didn't blow on the water's surface, but gulped it straight down, and their trunks, hanging down, continued drinking for a long time until they'd drunk their fill, which they announced with a grumble. The matriarch raised her trunk and let out another blast, at which they all raised their heads. The water-drinking session was finished, and the entire herd drew back in a tight formation around the watering hole at some distance from its edge. The mysterious moments of silence grew long as they stood in view of the water, as though they were expressing gratitude for that shimmering gift. Then they with-draw, walking backward, the way people withdrew when they took their leave from the courts of sultans and kings. They did not turn their backs to the water until they were some distance away from it; then the matriarch turned herself around, and in parallel with her, the whole herd turned. As a group, they halted for several minutes in a new period of silence. Then the matriarch moved, followed by the young mothers, the babies, and then the males who protect the rear of the convoy.

The elephants' water-drinking show took up two and a half hours, and as soon as the great, gray-black backs turned away, plunging into the thicket of trees and then disappearing in the distance, delayed exhaustion fell over us, and our fatigue made itself known. Feeling sleepy, I turned off to our hut, only to find that my colleague had gotten there ahead of me. I asked him if he had taken some good shots, and he replied that he'd taken a lot. Then we fell into a deep slumber.

We woke up with the sun in our eyes: the mid-day African sun was beating on the sanded glass of the hut's circular skylights near the roof. We were horrified to find that it was almost noon, since we were supposed to wake at seven, in order to have our breakfast and leave. Where was Katisha? Why didn't he come by, since he always woke up early? Five hours had passed, and our angry questions about his whereabouts turned into a genuine alarm about our being in this remote place without a guide, without Katisha. There were no telephone connections in this undeveloped wilderness, except via radio from the small station belonging to the Etosha National Park administration, which was reserved for emergency calls and transmissions in the event of disaster. We had some difficulty persuading the station official that our situation was dire, or that it demanded an emergency call.

In the evening, we succeeded in contacting the capital, Windhoek. We were frightened. Night fell on us with no sign of Katisha, and we didn't sleep well. We began to wait for the person that they told us would come to bring us back to the capital the next day, following the required investigation into the disappearance. The car was still in its spot in front of Katisha's empty hut. We gave our statements to a slender, young, Black investigator who bore a strong resemblance to Katisha. He kept trying to reassure us more than interrogate us. Then we left with the person who arrived to take us back to the capital, and in the same Land Rover that Katisha had driven us in.

Ten days into our stay in Namibia and no trace of Katisha had turned up. When I returned home on the fifteenth day I made a number of calls to Windhoek. Then a month after the trip, two months, three months, and even four months later, there was still no trace of Katisha. Two and half years later, at the Institute of African Studies in Cairo, I met a visiting professor from the University of Namibia. He told me that he was familiar with the incident of the disappearance of Katisha, who had not yet turned up, and was considered to be one of those who were lost in the wild.

Nine long years have passed, but I've never stopped going back over the group of photos from the Namibia trip. I am heartened by memories of the natural beauty in that pleasant land, but my feelings darken when I think about Katisha, who perished in the jaws of a nighttime predator, or by a daytime beast of prey. Nine years had to pass before I paused now, dumbfounded, before two photographs I had previously looked at hundreds of times without paying much attention to them. Two photos my colleague had taken during the night the elephants drank at the watering hole in Etosha:

The first photo shows the group of elephants facing forward, as they withdrew from the watering hole after drinking. There are twenty-two of them.

The second photo is of the same group of elephants after they had turned around, getting ready to head off. But this time there are twenty-three of them.

I go back and count again, and resort to a magnifying lens so as not to miscount, but I am certain that there is an extra elephant, and that this extra elephant is in the group of males on the right side of the semicircle of elephants returning to the wild. I can't explain it, except for production errors that occur when photos are developed, or so I've been told. But my photographer colleague rejects that idea, with all the vehemence of an experienced professional who doesn't appreciate my doubts about him knowing how to do his job.

Mohamed Makhzangi was born in Egypt's eastern Delta region in 1949. He trained as a physician, and in the 1970s he was imprisoned several times for his leftist political activities. In the mid-1980s, he lived in Kiev, where he studied psychology and alternative medicine: his experience in the Ukraine during the Chernobyl nuclear accident in 1986 formed the basis for a memoir published in English as *Memories of a Meltdown*. He practiced medicine for twelve years before turning to fiction and science journalism, in Kuwait and Cairo. His publications include several short story collections, two books of environmental fiction for children, and a nonfiction book about his travels in Asia. He is also a regular columnist for Egypt's daily newspaper *Al Shorouk*. In 1992 he won Egypt's Best Short Story Collection Award, and in 2005 he won the Sawiris Prize for Best Collection of Short Stories (Senior Authors).

Chip Rossetti has a PhD in modern Arabic literature from the University of Pennsylvania. His published translations of Arabic fiction include the novel *Beirut, Beirut* by Sonallah Ibrahim, the graphic novel *Metro: A Story of Cairo* by Magdy Elshafee, *Utopia* by Ahmed Khaled Towfik, and *Saint Theresa and Sleeping with Strangers* by Bahaa Abdelmeguid. His translations have also appeared in *New Voices of Arabia: The Short Stories—An Anthology from Saudi Arabia*, as well as on the website Words Without Borders. He has worked in book publishing for over twenty years, and is currently the editorial director for the Library of Arabic Literature series published by New York University Press.